I0591434

Metaphorosis

November 2021

Beautifully made speculative fiction

Also from Metaphorosis

Verdage

Reading 5X5 x2: Duets
Score – an SFF symphony
Reading 5X5: Readers' Edition
Reading 5X5: Writers' Edition

Metaphorosis Magazine

Metaphorosis: Best of 20xx
Metaphorosis 20xx: The Complete Stories
annual issues, from 2016

Monthly issues

Plant Based Press

Best Vegan Science Fiction & Fantasy
annual issues, from 2016

from B. Morris Allen:
Susurrus
Allenthology: Volume I
Tocsin: and other stories
Start with Stones: collected stories
Metaphorosis: a collection of stories

Metaphorosis

November 2021

edited by
B. Morris Allen

ISSN: 2573-136X (online)
ISBN: 978-1-64076-211-4 (e-book)
ISBN: 978-1-64076-212-1 (paperback)

Metaphorosis
a magazine of speculative fiction
from
Metaphorosis Publishing

Neskowin

November 2021

From the Editor

A lot of work goes into making a magazine, and much of it goes unrecognized. You know the authors of the stories — their name should follow the title of their story. You may know who the editor is — their name is usually mentioned somewhere. But there are a lot of others involved, and you don't usually hear about them — the assistant and associate editors, the podcast editor, the proofreader, the slush or second readers. They're doing a lot of the background work required to bring you good stories. And many of them (as at *Metaphorosis*) don't get paid a penny.

Many magazine staff are writers too — some first came to through stories we bought — but at *Metaphorosis*, we don't allow staff to submit to the magazine (with a gaping loophole that lets me, as editor, publish one of my own stories every year).

On the eve of our seventh year of publication, this issue is a special exception to the rule — an issue composed *only* of stories by long-time staff. It doesn't encompass all of our hard-working staff — people come and go, after all — but it does recognize some that have worked hard for us — and for you — for quite some time.

- A.J. Cunder has been one of our reliable Second Readers since early 2020.
- Matthew Gomez is been our indefatigable Podcast Editor and Host, making us sound good since fall 2019.
- J. Tynan Burke is our Assistant Editor and the Grand Elder of staff. "The Bagel Shop Owner's Nephew" was published in Metaphorosis August 2018.
- Jordan Chase-Young is our Proofreader and typo eradicator. His story "Shards" was published in Metaphorosis in July 2020.

Enjoy their work in *front* of the curtains for once!

Treedom

AJ Cunder

We were playing in the park when Garold first took root. We stopped kicking our ball and stared when Jack pointed to the man standing motionless in the middle of the grassy field.

"Isn't that the homeless guy who sleeps by the shrubbery?" Thomas asked in a whisper. "How long has he been like that?"

Like a tree that had just been planted, the homeless man's legs remained frozen, and we inched closer almost without realizing it, edging along the stream cutting through the park. He placed his arms at varying angles, adjusting the bend in his elbows, shifting—never lifting his feet—as though trying to find a natural position.

No one else in the small park spared him a second glance. Dogs preoccupied owners, joggers ran along trails that wound into the encroaching forest, parents collected kids from an old playground with wooden structures on the verge of collapse. A rusty merry-go-round squealed as loud as the children. Only the three of us, on the cusp of adolescence ourselves, paid the strange man any mind.

"Should we go up to him?" Jack's lips curled in a telltale grin. Always the adventurous one, he often inspired our quests—exploring the schoolhouse after dark, or pushing Thomas up his chimney to search for treasure. He took us to a lake once, describing jewels and gems hidden beneath the waters, but blushed when I stripped to my underwear. "Girls can't do that in front of boys," he insisted, but I ignored him and dove in.

"And do what?" Thomas asked, shoving hands in his pockets, glancing around as though planning an escape.

"Mr. Morton says in science class we need to be good observers of the world if we're going to learn anything." Jack rubbed his hands as though trying to start a fire. "What if the man's turned to stone? A living statue? What if Medusa is loose in the park?"

Thomas swallowed, and Jack said, "Come on, let's find out." He started walking with his determined stride, hopping from stone to stone across the stream.

Three meters from the man, we huddled together. His gray hair coiled like vines to his waist, and silver tags flashed from his neck. I gave a tentative wave, but the man's eyes never moved. His face was rough and leathery, almost like bark, the embroidered name on his jacket—G. AROLD—sprouting threads as time picked out the stitches.

"*Garold*," Jack said with a chuckle. Somehow, the word had a nice feel to it, the way it started in the back of the throat and rolled off the tongue.

Thomas whispered, "My mom tells me never to talk to strangers." He probably remembered his mother's scream when she had found him with his head up the chimney, covered in soot, and the corporal punishment that followed.

"We're not talking. We're watching," Jack said. "Mr. Morton—"

"I don't think he meant this." Thomas pushed his hands deeper into his jeans, as though trying to bury his forearms.

I slid my own hands along the pocketless fabric of my dress, searching for a place to slip my fingers. Not finding one, I fiddled with a strand of long hair my father rarely let me cut, fidgeting in the clothes he insisted I wear. "He looks harmless enough." I fished a granola bar from my backpack stash, often used to feed the squirrels and woodland creatures we encountered, and held it out to the man, who slowly extended his arm. Inching closer, I dropped the bar in his palm, searching his face for…something familiar, perhaps, a kindred spirit, even if I didn't quite recognize it at the time.

A bell tower tolled, and Thomas jumped. "Come on, let's go," he said. "Or I'll be late for dinner."

With a last look at the man standing in Grove Park, we crossed the rickety wooden bridge and split for home along the cobblestone roads.

When a week elapsed and Garold remained rooted like a scarecrow, the tiny Welsh town of Gwernogle took notice. Some tried to approach him, but he never said a word, always staring out to his own horizon. Thomas's mother wondered if it was safe to let her son play where an odd man might prey on children, but Thomas argued that Jack would be there to protect him. Jack's father gave him a Swiss Army knife and made sure he knew how to flip out the blade. My own father, the town's pastor, went to see the scene for himself. "How long has he been there, Ash?" he asked me.

"Almost a week, I think."

"The police should check on him. He could be ill," he reasoned.

A cruiser came, and an officer tried talking with Garold, asking if he needed an ambulance or a ride somewhere—but Garold only said, "I belong here," his voice like leaves rustling. He broke no laws by standing in a public park, so the officer scratched his head, scribbled some notes, and shrugged when my father asked what the police could do.

Our parents all but forbade us to play there, but of course we didn't listen. Garold's mystery became our mission, our chance to play detective, investigating the strange creature who claimed this space. Jack imagined finding fame and fortune, the prodigy child who had discovered the first living statue. Thomas pretended to be a scientist, proposing hypotheses and theories, examining the soil around Garold's feet, taking samples and extracting conjectures—what kept him there? How did he survive? When would he leave? And I was a philosopher, wondering what it meant for Garold to stand there each day, unmoving, rooted to the ground, a singularity, a blip in the otherwise uniform grass that had grown for countless years undisturbed. The town groundskeeper grumbled at first, his routine altered. But finally he began mowing around Garold, who never shifted even as the ancient, roaring machine approached. Soon, the grass grew around his feet, swallowing his boots with their holes near the toe.

A week later, we were still no closer to solving Garold's mystery. I offered him another granola bar as we gathered around him, the only souls besides Garold in the heart of the park. Most of the other children, after spying Garold frozen in his eternal vigil, would abandon the swings and playground to the ravens keeping watch among the metal bars and plastic towers.

We never saw Garold ingest what I gave him, and no wrappers littered the ground.

"What do you think he eats?" I wondered. "Or drinks?"

"Maybe other people bring him food? And water?" Thomas wondered, sitting in the grass. He held up a hand to shield his eyes from the sun even as thunderclouds approached. "Should've brought glasses," he said as Garold slowly moved an arm. We froze, watching him, until he stopped, his hand between Thomas and the sun, a thin shadow falling across Thomas's eyes.

When Garold stilled, Jack continued notching a stick with his knife. "Maybe he absorbs nutrients from the ground, like a tree."

At this, Garold slowly turned his head. He smiled a deliberate, crooked smile, his few remaining teeth jutting from chapped lips. "You understand," he said, dry as kindling.

Jack jumped at the sound, eyebrows raised, and Thomas scuttled behind him.

"Understand what?" Jack asked, smoothing his blonde-streaked hair, shrugging off his moment of skittishness.

Garold nodded. "Like a tree." We glanced at each other, and he shuddered, holding his silver army tags to his nose and squinting. He pulled on the chain until it was taut, in danger of snapping, but then he exhaled and slumped, the tags falling against his chest.

The first drops of a coming storm splashed our foreheads. "Come on," Thomas said. "We're gonna get soaked if we don't leave." He tugged on Jack's sleeve, who looked for a moment like he'd pull away.

"What about him?" I asked, a sudden spark tingling in my gut, an itch spreading through thoughts that had long swirled inside me. *Like a tree*, he had said. *Like a tree*. I pulled at a strap of my dress, resisting the urge to slip it off, to emerge from the wrappings that defined me, marked me as *girl*.

"If he doesn't want to get drenched, he'll move too," Jack said.

A thunderclap shook us to the bone like a bomb detonating, and Garold's face twisted as he shuddered. He raised his arms over his head as an unkindness of ravens croaked nearby.

We ran—but Thomas turned back and draped his poncho over Garold, quickly, as though afraid to stay in contact with him for too long.

"Come on!" Jack yelled. "I'm not waiting for you."

We didn't stay to see if Garold took shelter when the rain came, but the next day he stood, same as the days before, Thomas's poncho still slung over his shoulders.

When complaints came to city hall, the town council made their own inquiries with the Gwernogle police. The chief offered her apologies, but despite all biological laws, Garold didn't exhibit any physical distress. He only ever said, "I belong here," when officers approached, and even if parents feared for their children's safety, the police had no probable cause to forcibly remove him.

So the council of seven hosted a town hall which, despite our parents' reservations, we attended.

"It's just not normal," the townspeople said, fifty of Gwernogle's three-hundred residents crammed into the old stone inn that had for centuries served as the gathering place for official business. Gas lamps flickered along the walls—while most of the town had reasonably reliable electricity, the inn was so old that any renovations would risk bringing it down completely. "What kind of person stands in the middle of a park all day? Our kids are afraid to go there. We have to stay with them or drive them all the way to Brechfa to play."

From their lofty bench, the council of seven dark suits looked down upon those gathered. They added, "It certainly is strange, and we've had our police department out to investigate. Clearly, they have been inadequate in resolving the problem. We aren't quite sure why he's there or what he's doing, and none of the officers have been able to figure it out either. A concern we must address with their leader." They glanced at the police chief, who frowned as she hovered near the exit.

I stared at my fingers, imagining them to be roots, tendrils to penetrate rock and soil. I swallowed and raised my hand.

"Yes? Young lady in the back, you have something to say?" the council asked, faces pale even in the flickering orange light.

I stood and plucked at my dress, envying Thomas's jeans, Jack's dark jacket, their short hair, the stubble that would soon sprout on their chins. I felt my own smooth cheeks, folding arms over a budding chest as Jack raised an eyebrow, Thomas's knee just touching his, Jack letting it stay there.

I took a breath and said, "He is a tree. He told us."

A few chuckles bounced around the room, along with "absurd" and "ridiculous."

"Young lady," the council said, "he is clearly a man, not a tree. Whatever delusions he may have, he cannot remain a permanent fixture of our park. It simply isn't right to behave in such a manner."

"Unsightly. Frightening," some townspeople chimed in. "Unnatural."

Thomas's forearms disappeared in his pockets—how I wished I had pockets of my own—and he muttered something under his breath, shifting his leg away from Jack's.

I started to sit, but then straightened and added, "*He* says he's a tree. Wouldn't he know?"

No one answered, though the adults looked to one another, a hint of fear shading their eyes, distrust of anything that disturbed the norms settled for centuries upon this small, isolated town in the middle of the Welsh countryside.

After little more discussion, the council instituted a curfew in Grove Park that would take effect the following night. The police chief received her commission: anyone in the park between 11 PM and 6 AM must be ordered to vacate the property.

The town groundskeeper made hasty signs and posted them at the park's entrances. We considered tearing them down, but decided instead to sit with Garold when the police came. It was an opportunity to express ourselves, to lash out against the establishment, whatever that meant, to fight for something even if we didn't entirely know what exactly we were fighting for. Or perhaps we did, in some subterranean part of us; a seed had been planted, taking root in our minds. When I saw Garold, I recognized in him something I had long tried to hide within myself, a search for self-identity amidst a sense of disconnectedness, a sense of unbelonging. I kept this from the others, though. They didn't need to know. Not everything. Not just yet.

Thomas, of course, nearly stayed home, citing a stomach ache, but Jack threw pebbles at his window and promised to keep at it until Thomas finally snuck out the back. I stocked my backpack with snacks, and Jack brought a flashlight and rope so we could tie ourselves together around Garold—if it came to that.

We got there before the police, but not before the ravens, who shuffled along the edge of the park where the border blended into the forest. They croaked and flapped their wings as a crowd began to gather, spectators carrying electric lanterns. "Is that Jimmy?" Jack asked, spotting our classmate, captain of the football team.

"Yeah, I think it is," I said, waving to Jimmy who raised a hand in return.

"Come on over!" Jack called. But Jimmy ignored him, his parents clutching his shoulders.

A sudden chill bit through our clothes, and we shivered, a quick glance passing between us. "Is this really a good idea?" Thomas asked.

"Of course it is," Jack said. His hand darted like a fox, so quick I might have missed it if I hadn't been looking. Even so, I blinked and wondered if I really had seen him squeeze Thomas's hand.

"I belong here," Garold kept repeating to no one in particular, the grass at his feet now reaching past his knees, blending so thoroughly it became difficult to discern where his body ended and the earth began.

When the police arrived at 10:45 PM, they issued a warning, shining their spotlights at Garold. "As per local ordinance," the sergeant said, "Grove Park shall close to visitors at eleven each night. Sir, we are giving you a lawful order to leave now or face legal consequences." The sergeant looked at us as though just noticing we were there. "What are you kids doing? Go on, get home now. Where are your parents?" He looked to the crowd interspersed along the tree line.

"We're not leaving," Jack said. "We won't let you take him."

The sergeant shined his light in Jack's face. "Come on, now, no sense getting mixed up in this. How old are you, twelve, thirteen? You really want a police record?"

Jack dropped to the ground at Garold's feet—Thomas too, though sweat started to bead on his brow, and I followed. We leaned against Garold's legs and wrapped the rope around ourselves.

"Sarge? Should we take them all?" one of the patrol officers asked.

"Wait till they fall asleep, then we'll take the tree man. Can't be long, they'll knock out soon enough. And see if we've gotten any calls about missing children."

But we didn't fall asleep. We stayed up long after the crowd of townspeople dispersed, long after the officers finished their fourth cups of coffee, with the ravens still watching like silent sentinels. "All right kids," the sergeant finally said. "You win. Why don't you let us take you home, and we'll leave this man alone?"

"Thank God," Thomas said, starting to shrug off the rope when Jack grabbed his arm.

"Wait. First, this *man* is a *tree*. Second, how do we know you're telling the truth?" Jack asked, his eyes narrowing.

"You'll just have to trust us, kid," the sergeant sighed.

"I think we'll wait until morning when you can't make him leave. Six AM, right?"

The sergeant ground his teeth, and the standoff continued.

We took turns sleeping. The police did the same, with nothing else they could do short of ripping us bodily away. Garold stood as he always stood.

When a gray haze lightened the sky, our parents found us in the park after we didn't appear for breakfast and they discovered our empty beds. Perhaps they should've been more concerned, but it was Gwernogle after all, and nothing bad ever happened here. Jack's dad only chuckled and praised his son's rope work. "I taught him that knot," he said to the sergeant who checked his watch.

Nevertheless, Thomas's mother gasped, "What on Earth were you thinking?" She reached for his hand, but he wriggled away. "Thomas, what are you doing? Come with me this instant." She looked at Garold and frowned. "Thomas. Right now. Come with me."

My father stared at the ground, rubbing his chin.

"I'm not leaving!" I called out, and he scowled.

"Thomas, you have to go to school. Come with your mother. Come right now." Her glasses trembled dangerously on the bridge of her nose. "Stop this madness."

"Tell them to stop." Thomas nodded to the police, fingers wrapped around Jack's wrist, eyes widening as though surprised at his own boldness.

"Okay," the sergeant said.

"Really?" Thomas squeaked.

"Six AM. Curfew's over. Until tonight, anyway. We'll be back."

"And so will we!" Jack yelled between yawns.

Our parents tried to stop us. My father threatened to ground me, lock me in my room, take away my spotty internet. But I insisted I'd climb out the window. "Ashley, what's gotten into you?" he asked, running fingers through his hair. "You were always a well-behaved girl. Why this sudden change?"

"Maybe it's not so sudden," I offered, before my voice withered. *Maybe I've never felt comfortable as your little girl*, I wanted to say, *as the perfect pastor's perfect daughter. Maybe this skin isn't really my own.* But of course, I only looked down as he tapped his fingers on the counter.

Thomas's mother outlined the dangers, some more likely than others, and listed the health effects of improper sleep. But he shook his head, and said, "Jack will be there."

"You do everything with that boy," his mother said, frowning. "If he walked off a cliff, you'd follow him." And Thomas didn't deny it.

Jack's own father gave him sleeping bags and water canteens, and showed him more sophisticated knots.

Unable to contain us, our parents came on the second night of our vigil and watched on the wooden bridge beside the ravens, wary of violating the curfew themselves. When the police arrived, they brandished their nightsticks. One officer spun his like a propeller, and it whistled through the air. They tried half-heartedly to untie the rope that bound us, and Garold stiffened more than usual at their approach; but we covered the knots with our hands, our bodies, Thomas's arms wrapped around Jack's waist, and eventually the police gave up, retreating to their cruisers, where they sipped coffee and joked about worse ways to pass a night shift.

On the third night, the council of seven appeared in their raven-black suits, faces like ghouls in the lamplight. "Sergeant," they said. "Why is this man still here?" Birds cackled in the trees, a murder of crows circling over Garold's head.

The sergeant nodded towards us. "He's attracted some sympathy from the youth."

The council hovered over us like shades of Hades. "If they are a problem, Sergeant, then remove them as well," they said.

The sergeant laughed. "Right. And when the local paper runs a story about the police abducting children in the park, you lot will be the first to call for our resignation. I'd like to keep my job, thank you."

The council scowled, and they conferred with one another. Then, as one, they reached for our rope. The ravens fluttered their wings.

"I wouldn't do that," the sergeant said, tapping his nightstick.

"And why not?" the council hissed.

"Well, you see, since you're not officers of the law, if you lay a hand on these children, then that would be battery. Something I just couldn't turn my back on."

The council looked for a moment like they might do it anyway, and we held our breath, eyeing the ravens that hopped closer. Thomas grabbed Jack's arm and squeezed. But Garold rested his hands on our shoulders and stared at the council, acorn eyes boring into theirs of obsidian.

Without another word, the council of seven withdrew into the darkness, and the ravens along with them.

"Think they'll be back?" one of the officers asked.

The sergeant shrugged. "Let's hope not. Can't say I appreciate when those devils tell me how to do my work."

On the fourth night, we found a case of water by Garold when we arrived, along with a bag of chips and a container of homemade casserole. On the fifth night, our classmate Jimmy shuffled up and asked if he could join us. His parents screamed from the park's border, but he stood resolute, his back turned to them, eyes cautiously darting between Jack and Thomas. "You two, are you..." he couldn't seem to finish the sentence, but I knew what he meant. I think we all knew.

"Sit with us," I offered. "We won't turn you away. Garold certainly won't."

On the sixth night, Mr. Morton came with a notebook. "Fascinating," he'd mutter occasionally, asking us questions, trying to interview Garold who never said much, other than, "I belong here, as a tree. No, not a man. A *tree.*" Mr. Morton stared, once, when Thomas's pinky overlapped with Jack's on the ground, frowning at first, but then twisting his lips in what might have been the beginning of a smile.

On the sixth night, we insisted that our parents sit with us. At first they stood a ways off, apologizing repeatedly to the police, who just sipped their coffee. But we grabbed their hands and brought them closer. We introduced them to Garold, who ever so slightly nodded his head.

"May I ask, sir, what it is you're doing here?" Thomas's mother dusted off her sleeve. Perhaps she saw the way her son's foot tapped against Jack's. Perhaps she chose to ignore it.

"I belong here," Garold rustled. "Should have been planted here instead of mother's womb. I should wear bark on branches, grow leaves, not hair. Drop acorns, not..." His lips tightened, and he tugged on his army tags until the chain nearly broke.

I fidgeted—but this night, with jeans borrowed from Thomas's wardrobe, I had something underneath, something between my skin and the scratchy wool of my father's dress. Thomas never questioned why I wanted them, when I asked for a pair, just handed them over and said I'd probably look better in them than he did.

Garold's eyes shifted like roots searching for purchase, and caught her gaze. "Do you believe that I belong?"

"Oh," Thomas's mother answered, glancing away. "I suppose we all belong, don't we? One way or another."

Garold slowly smiled.

On the seventh night, Jimmy brought the rest of the football team. They came at first to see the novelty—and because the school's star athlete told them to. But then something shifted; around Garold, we all seemed to find a sense of belonging, near this man-who-was-a-tree, where normativity began to fray around the edges—if we could accept this, what couldn't we accept?

Our nightly protest slowly transformed. People came at first to see what the whole town talked about, but then stayed for the fellowship, where conversations bonded strangers around bonfires, the community gathered with Garold at its center. Those who were more vocally inclined offered entertainment, and even the police partook of the homemade pies and dishes that went around.

Folk began asking Garold where he came from, if he had any family, but he never said much other than "I belong here." Then they started asking why he thought he was a tree.

Jack intervened, holding up a finger. "No, no, no. He doesn't *think* he's a tree. He *is* a tree."

In that moment, my heart sang. I added, "He's probably never felt comfortable in his own skin. It's not like bark. It's too soft." He closed his eyes and hummed as I spoke. "The world moves too fast for him. Trees, they take it slow. This is where he belongs. The world doesn't feel wrong, here. He doesn't feel wrong." I wound a coil of hair around my finger. "Like me."

The townspeople nodded—perhaps they didn't hear those last words lost to the wind, or didn't know quite how to process them, their heads tilted slightly to the side as they said, "That's nice," and moved on to other conversation.

A fortnight after our first vigil, Jack asked, as he stood watch over Garold—still wary of the police, still fingering the Swiss knife in his pocket—"Do you think they've finally accepted him?"

"Who?" I asked, trying to coax a shrew towards me with a handful of oats as someone in the crowd sang "*Suo Gan.*"

"The town. The adults."

Thomas shrugged, hands eternally in his pockets. "Seems like they're warming up, at the least."

"I meant, *accepted* who?"

"Oh. Garold, of course."

My thoughts flashed to the scissors sitting on my dresser back home, their gleam in the lamplight, my own visage in the mirror, the glint in Thomas's eyes when he looked at Jack, my father's preaching on Sunday. I searched the crowd for my father's face and caught him laughing with Thomas's mother, nodding in our direction, throwing us a smile and wave.

He came over, a package tucked under his arm, bringing Thomas's mother and Jack's father with him. "Hello, Garold," he said as he approached, hefting the brown paper. "We, uh… the three of us got you something." He held out the gift, but Garold made no move to accept it. So my father untied the strings, stripped off the wrappings and waved a denim jacket with embroidery like vines running down the sleeves. Garold's face brightened, even in the shadows cast by the fires, and Thomas's mother helped him shed his old skin, disturbing the squirrel perched on his shoulder.

"You didn't have to," I said to my dad. "But thanks."

He squeezed my shoulder, and that morning, before catching a moment of sleep, I slipped my hair between the shears and cut it, strands floating to the floor like leaves. When breakfast time came, I stood at the top of the steps, waiting to descend, taking a breath, remembering Garold. Each step felt like I carried a millstone, but foot by foot, I dragged myself to the table. My father looked up from his coffee mug, ran his eyes over my head, but said nothing, only swallowed once and finished his meal.

When Jack and Thomas saw me at school, they gaped for a moment, but then punched my shoulder. "New look, huh?" Jack said, his cheeks slightly reddening. "Maybe I'll try on one of your dresses tomorrow."

"Do it," I teased. "I've already got a pair of Thomas's jeans I'm going to wear."

When Garold saw me later that day, his smile cracked through leathered skin wider than I'd ever seen before, like a split in bark that could never close again. "You understand," he said, though I wasn't quite sure, this time, what he meant.

Garold's newfound smile brightened his face even as children sat under his shade to escape the sun, or swung from his arm as they might a branch, little boys climbing to sit on his shoulders beside robins and bluejays, pointing out and laughing as though they had scaled the tallest tree in the world. Ravens occasionally watched us from the edge of the park, brooding, but they never came close.

The council quietly rescinded their ordinance, and the following night, at the Treedom Rally, as our gatherings had come to be known, the police assured us Garold would be left to conduct his business in whatever manner he wished.

"I still don't trust them," Jack said, even as the townspeople cheered and congratulated Garold. "We should stay, just in case."

But we were tired—we were ready for a night of sleep in our own beds. So we didn't stay. Perhaps we should have, because the next morning, Garold was gone. His clothes remained—boots with chipmunks nestled inside, jacket spread upon the grass—and a sapling rose where he had once stood, the soil churned at its base as though someone had just planted it. The disturbed ground was oblong and the length of a man, but none of us mentioned that aloud.

Jack bent over and picked something out of the dirt. "His army tags," he said, holding them up to the sun.

We protested at the police station, but they insisted they hadn't taken him. The town council similarly held up their hands and shrugged. We tried to form a search party, but our parents said he had likely just moved on, that he must have found whatever he was looking for. No one bothered to dig up the sapling, to see what lay beneath it.

In the park, we ringed Garold's sapling with stones big enough, high enough, to mark it as sacred, a barrier against the town groundskeeper, who grumbled each time he passed our shrine. It would remain a testament to Garold, a monument, we reasoned. We would ensure Gwernogle never forgot.

Jack scratched *Garold* into one of the rocks with his knife, adding, *who is a tree*, while I left a handful of granola so the birds and squirrels would come. Thomas bowed his head and said something that might have been a prayer, though we had never taken him as spiritually inclined. I laid a hand on the bark still supple and soft and a tingle shot up my arm, up the sleeve of Thomas's shirt I had borrowed, through my body, across the jeans so wonderfully scratchy and tight on my legs. Suddenly, I knew. "He did it," I breathed. "It's him. He never left."

Jack scoffed, but then he felt the bark too, and his eyes widened. In a flash, he nodded, then hugged Thomas, pecked him quickly on the cheek. Thomas wiped his face at first, glancing around, but then touched a finger to the sapling and nodded too. It didn't make sense—not logically, anyway, not according to the laws of biology or science. But it did make sense in the same strange way that faith makes sense, even when reason or convention say otherwise.

We tried to guess what kind of tree it might be, but of course we were no experts in dendrology. The nascent green shoots might have been oak, as Jack suggested, or willow, as Thomas believed, or even maple, as I supposed. We hung Garold's tags at the sapling's peak, where they still rest to this day, never bothered by ravens. And whenever we have moments of doubt, or uncertainty, we visit Garold and climb his branches, pulling ourselves to the top where we sit beside robins and cardinals, Jack and Thomas hand in hand, my own legs clad in jeans. From that height, we look out on the town, the twinkle of new electric light shining through the old stone inn and the shrinking flock of ravens who linger on it.

See A.J. Cunder's story "Treedom" online at Metaphorosis.
If you liked it, leave a comment. Authors love that!
Remember to subscribe to our e-mail updates so you'll know when new stories are posted.

About the story

The concept for this piece emerged from my own struggles with "fitting in," and finding acceptance as a member of the gay community. At first, Garold was meant to embody this transformation, while the children were mostly just observers—conduits between Garold and the town. But after a few rounds of edits, I realized (along with Morris) that the true heart of this story centered around the three children and their interaction with Garold—how he is able to change them—first, to accept their true selves, and second, to help a conservative town at least begin to consider (if not embrace) self-identities that disrupt deeply ingrained normative values. And I wanted the piece to accomplish this by pushing the concept of self-identity beyond LGBTQIA+ to explore what it means to know one's self even in a way no one else can. I hope, at least in some small way, this story can participate in the critical dialogue ongoing in our society that will one day produce a world of acceptance, no matter the clothes we wear, the bodies we inhabit, or the love we share.

A question for the author

Q: If your writing style were a bird, what type of bird would it be and why?

A: My first instinct when I saw this was to say "raven" because of how prominently they're featured in "Treedom". However, I posed this question to the writers group I frequently attend and one member, after careful consideration, suggested that my writing style most appropriately compares to a swan. She explained that swans are both elegant and fierce, mysterious and passionate, light and dark. I think that's a nearly perfect summation of my writing style —at the sentence level, I aim for graceful language with the power to evoke deep emotion; in terms of plot, I often find myself discovering the mysteries of a story as I write it (I seldom plan out anything in advance); and I would certainly agree that my stories tend to balance light and dark aspects, striving for a hopeful note but at the same time acknowledging the grim realities that so often face humanity.

About the author

A.J. Cunder is a Second Reader for Metaphorosis

A medievalist, a type 1 diabetic, and a cyber crime investigator, A.J. graduated from Seton Hall University with a Masters in Creative Writing after getting his Bachelors in English and Philosophy. Hobbies that occupy his spare time include sword fighting, playing the piano, learning the viola, running, hiking, spoiling his husky, and, of course, writing. He currently serves on the editorial staff of *Flash Fiction Online, Cosmic Roots & Eldritch Shores*, and *Metaphorosis*.

  www.WrestlingTheDragon.com, @aj_cunder

Right Behind You

Matthew Gomez

Surface

Carlos sat in the grav-lift, the orange light of sodium lamps pushing through his closed eyelids. He imagined the light was a sunrise back home in El Salvador and that he was sitting next to his wife and daughter at their kitchen table. He smelled fried plantains and charred pupusas instead of the stale air recirculating through his exo-suit. With concentration, he could reach out and run his fingers through his wife's hair, put his hand on his daughter's tiny shoulder—a memory he cherished. One he *didn't* mind reliving again and again.

He savored the illusion until his new partner settled into the grav-lift bench opposite him, and Carlos's comms filled with the familiar, incessant crackle of a Geiger counter. At ground-level, the device emitted the quiet static of a radio losing reception. As the grav-lift surged downward, carrying Carlos and his partner deeper into the hot zone, the Geiger counter's crackle grew. The orange glow of the lights strobed as the cart picked up speed, and Carlos's imagination faltered. He was no longer in El Salvador, but heading for the reactor meltdown the cart carried them toward.

Once touted as the answer to North America's energy crisis, the underground reactor had been built close enough to the Pacific to pipe in water for cooling but far enough underground it would be sequestered from any natural disasters that might disturb its cores. In the unlikely event that something went wrong, its builders promised, the reactors would stay safe.

The promise had held for six months.

During the first seismic rumblings of the Great Quakes, managers at the reactor smiled and congratulated themselves on the facility's safety. When those rumblings grew into earth-shattering quakes, cracking the ground open like the surface of a dried lakebed, the whole western hemisphere risked radioactive poisoning. It was why Carlos and hundreds of other immigrant workers just like him now found themselves tunneling through a mountain of underground rock to install a containment barrier.

"You drill where we say, and we plug up the holes," a bored engineer had said to Carlos during orientation nearly two years ago. "Do what we say, and you'll stay safe. Before you know it, you'll be holding a green card and can put all this behind you."

Carlos, yanked from his memory of home by the Geiger counter's hissing crackle, opened his eyes in annoyance. "Turn that fucking thing off," he said in Spanish, looking through the dense glass of his visor into the brown eyes of his young partner.

The kid obediently moved his hand to his wrist console, but he paused. Sweat beaded on his forehead, his eyes wide with nerves like a rabbit surveying the sky over an open field. "The foreman told us to leave it on," he responded, his accent familiar. "Said it's a safety regulation."

"It's annoying and useless," Carlos said. "We're descending toward a nuclear meltdown. There's radiation—lots of it. Now turn it off."

The Geiger counters were one of many supposed safety protocols meant to protect the workers. They were there for show, just like the air circulators, bulky med kits, and alarms conspicuously placed in the tunnels below. If a collapse occurred or the reactor faced some unexpected explosion, none of it would save the workers. The only equipment that mattered was the exo-suits Carlos and his partner wore. With hydraulic joints, embedded lead plating, and powerful filters, they were the only thing separating the workers from the radioactive air in the tunnels.

The kid obeyed and turned off his Geiger counter. The crackle playing through Carlos's comms was replaced by the kid's rapid, shallow breathing and the whir of air rushing past their bulky exo-suits.

The sound reminded Carlos of the swelling panic he'd felt *his* first time down.

The orange lamps had illuminated the tunnel ahead, but it might as well have been a black hole drawing him toward inevitable doom. Only time and repetition made things easier, but those first dozen trips down were hell. Carlos didn't feel bad about putting the kid in his place, but he needed to play nice for now, or his plan would fall apart before it really got started.

"We're going to be fine," Carlos said, working to subdue the grit in his voice. "I know it's your first time down, but I've done it hundreds of times. We'll be back surface-side before you know it."

"It doesn't seem worth it," the kid said, his voice cracking. "I shouldn't have come."

Carlos shook his head. As dangerous as the excavation work was, it was worth it. Signing up had bought him and his family temporary US citizenship, with the promise of full citizenship after he completed his contract. His wife and daughter were in family housing 1,500 miles away in Texas, safe from the violent gangs that had run them out of El Salvador. Carlos had gladly traded the risks of the excavation for the extortion he faced back home. Anything to protect his family.

"Do what I say, and you'll be fine," Carlos grunted. He hoped the confidence in his voice was enough to mask his intentions—mask the plan he'd set in motion when he selected the kid as his partner.

After so many trips down, the rebreather on Carlos's exo-suit was beginning to fail, which was a death sentence for someone that spent the bulk of each day in subterranean tunnels over a radioactive meltdown. He'd tried going to the foreman for a replacement, but he'd burned that bridge long ago, which left Carlos only one other option: take one for himself.

Finding the kid—his mark—had been easy. At the first sign of his rebreather filter failing, Carlos had started hanging around the shuttle drop-off at the main gate of the workers' camp. Every evening he'd watched new recruits spill out of their gleaming metal shuttles, looking for the crown tattoo that would ease his conscience. He didn't need to know anything else about his victim. The mark of the gang that had driven him here was enough. Carlos's whole body had trembled when he saw the kid emerge from the shuttle, the crown tattoo on his forehead peeking out from behind black bangs. He was younger than Carlos had hoped for, but the boy's hard expression conveyed the exact violence Carlos had run from. The kid was young, but that didn't make him innocent.

Carlos's wrist console beeped a warning about his rebreather filter as the grav-lift continued its descent, and he slapped it quiet with a gloved hand.

"What was that?" the kid asked.

"Your accent sounds familiar," Carlos responded, ignoring the question. "Salvadoran?"

The kid looked up, his tense expression easing. "Guatemalan."

"What's your name?"

"Miguel," the kid mumbled.

"I'm Carlos. We're going to be fine. Just breathe."

"You've really been down hundreds of times?" Miguel asked.

"It'll be two years in a few weeks, and I'll be finished."

"Guess you know what you're doing."

Carlos nodded. Playing nice with the kid took more restraint than he had expected. For the first time since Carlos had spotted Miguel, they were close enough that Carlos could reach out, wrap his reinforced fingers around Miguel's throat until his body went limp, then strip his suit of its new rebreather filter—all before they reached the bottom of the grav-lift track. But then he'd be left with a body and no way to get rid of the evidence. That wouldn't do. If he were caught, his shot at citizenship would disintegrate, so instead he clenched his jaw, gripped the edge of the cart to steady his trembling hands, and focused on the gentle sway of the grav-lift, ruminating on the real work ahead of him.

1,000 Feet

A red light flashed ahead, illuminating a reflective placard glowing through a fine coating of dust: *1,000 feet below surface.*

"Is all the housing as bad as mine, or do they stick the new guys in the worst units?" Miguel asked, tapping through a series of menus on his wrist console.

The fidgeting reminded Carlos of the way his daughter distracted herself with her favorite toy: a pink plastic horse, the joints of its limbs worn loose. The memory peeled open the hurt he felt from being away for so long and flared up the anger he'd been working to subdue. If it weren't for *Los Reyes*, the gang comprised of countless vicious punks just like Miguel, he'd be home and able to see his daughter —wrap her up in his arms until she giggled and squirmed free.

"What do you think?" Carlos spat.

Miguel looked up, his eyebrows knitted. "Sorry, just wondering."

Play nice, Carlos reminded himself, a sigh creeping past his lips. "They're all shitholes. Just enough to keep the weather out and our stink in. Everyone's too exhausted at the end of a shift to bother cleaning."

"Doesn't the foreman say anything?"

Just the mention of the foreman made Carlos's hands tighten into fists. The guy was a sociopath. When he felt particularly irritable, Carlos liked to imagine what he might do if he found himself in a locked room with the guy.

"He couldn't care less. To him and everyone else running this mess we're just bodies. They call us 'backs' when they think we're not listening."

" 'Backs'?"

Carlos twisted to the side and tapped a reinforced finger against the flexible section of exo-suit covering his back. "It's all they think we're good for in this country—we're strong and we'll do the work their poor won't touch. It's always been that way here. Ask the Chinese in the 1800s. Ask our great-grandparents and their parents, who picked crops for American stomachs. Ask *our parents*, who built the desalinization plants off the coast when the rivers dried up. Then ask yourself what the foreman thinks of you."

"I don't care what the foreman thinks as long as I get mine," Miguel said.

Typical, Carlos thought. "You should," he said. "You give your humanity to someone like the foreman, and you'll never get it back."

Carlos knew from experience. Soon after he'd started, he'd gone to the foreman to complain about a number of broken safety regulations he'd witnessed: tunnelers like himself working without scanners to get more done in less time and areas not being cordoned off properly during excavations, to name just a couple. The foreman made it clear that results were all that mattered.

"If you're that upset about how I'm running things here, you can go back to your shithole country," the foreman had said. The auto-translator box on the foreman's desk leeched the venom from his tone as it spat out the words in a monotone Spanish, but Carlos got the point. "No one's forcing you to stay here. Last thing I need is another *back* that doesn't know how to keep his fuckin' mouth shut."

Back then, Carlos had thought the foreman had to be an anomaly. Not everyone could be so careless about regulations, not with so many lives at risk. So he waited, keeping a tally of the broken safety measures until he could tell someone who would actually listen.

He'd found his chance at the end of a shift in the tunnels when he ran across a group of officials wrapping up one of their regular inspections. They were gathered at the equipment check-out stands and stood out like black flies in a bowl of crema. Their gloved fingers were too clean and their postures too upright. The heaviest thing they'd lifted that day were the tablets they scribbled on as they moved through the hot zone.

Carlos had walked up, tapped one on the shoulder, and begun the speech he'd been running through his head since his conversation with the foreman. The officials translated Carlos's statement with their tablets, nodding along as he spoke. When he finished, he noticed one of the officials shaking his head and chuckling to himself. Carlos couldn't figure out why. And it wasn't until he woke up the next morning being shaken awake by the foreman that he understood. The officials hadn't taken their findings to any regulators at higher offices of government. They'd taken it straight to the foreman.

Carlos could still remember the expression on the foreman's face as he'd leaned over him, his face blood red. Without an auto-translator, Carlos didn't understand what the foreman was muttering, but he knew it wasn't good. The foreman didn't yell, which made the even cadence of his words even more terrifying.

Carlos had hoped the foreman might eventually forget, but that was wishful thinking at best, willful ignorance at worst. That foreman's ability to hold a grudge had proved stronger than Carlos expected, and he regretted ever thinking he could make a difference.

"It's worth it, though," Miguel said, snapping Carlos back to the present. "Land of opportunity and all." The kid's optimism was an annoying reminder of how Carlos had felt when he'd signed on.

Carlos scoffed. "It better be." Suddenly he was the one breathing hard.

"You seem too smart for this."

The compliment caught Carlos off-guard. He liked it better when the kid fit the gangster image Carlos had crafted in his head. He shifted uncomfortably in the cart. "I studied history back home. Wanted to be a teacher."

"Why this, then?"

Carlos clenched his jaw, replaying for the thousandth time in his head his final interaction with *Los Reyes*—the reason he'd fled with his wife and daughter to the United States. "There weren't any other options."

"It was that bad in El Salvador?"

"We're going almost two miles underground to excavate tunnels above a nuclear meltdown. Yeah. It was really bad."

Miguel nodded.

"You know that tattoo won't do you any favors if you live long enough to get citizenship," Carlos said before the kid could ask another stupid question.

Miguel reached up, putting a gloved hand against the lead glass of his visor, his fingers massaging the spot directly over the crown. For the first time since he'd sat across from Carlos, Miguel seemed to run out of things to say.

Carlos's wrist console beeped, and he slapped it silent once more.

"Something wrong with your suit?" Miguel asked, dropping his hand to his lap.

"It's fine," Carlos lied. He'd gone to the foreman for a replacement a month ago, but as Carlos was explaining the problems with his suit, the foreman lifted a hand to silence him, took a deep breath, then leaned in close to the auto-translator.

"Damn thing seems to be on the fritz," the foreman said, his words translated into perfect Spanish. He slapped the speaker with false irritation. "Everything you're saying is coming out garbled."

The foreman flicked the power switch off, and the auto-translator went dead. He pointed a finger at Carlos. With the auto-translator off, Carlos didn't understand what the foreman said next, but the expression he wore—the sweat beading on his red face—was enough to let Carlos know he wasn't getting a new rebreather filter.

Every breath since then felt borrowed, another grain of sand dropped from the dwindling top of an hourglass. He kicked at the silt-covered bottom of the grav-lift and wondered how much radioactive dust he'd inhale when his rebreather finally stopped working. He wondered how long he'd live afterward. He wondered if he'd live long enough to see his family again if it came to that.

The exo-suit suddenly felt too small, too cramped, and Carlos's pulse throbbed in his neck. A shiver ran down his back, and he grew lightheaded as anxiety surged its way through his body. Holding his breath, Carlos looked up, afraid Miguel might have sensed something odd about the sudden silence.

Miguel was fiddling with the console on his wrist, the light from its panel illuminating the rebreather jutting from his chest—the one containing a fresh set of filters. Carlos's eyes locked onto the rebreather. Only then did his shoulders relax, and the painful knot in his chest begin to loosen.

7,000 Feet

The sub-surface air pumping into Carlos's exo-suit grew warmer the further they descended, the collapsed radioactive cores dumping heat into the network of tunnels like a raging furnace.

To pass the time and hopefully stave off his swelling anxiety, Carlos scanned his exo-suit for damage, running his fingers over the thousands of scrapes and dings that scarred its metal exterior. Despite the countless abrasions, the suit still functioned. It kept the radiation out, and its hydraulic pistons multiplied the output of his well-toned muscles. Without a new rebreather filter, though, the suit would be little more than a walking coffin, which the foreman had made clear was no concern of his. Carlos didn't need the auto-translator to know that if he died in the suit, the foreman would have a line of other "backs" eager to stuff themselves inside it.

Carlos had gone to some of the partners he'd worked with to see if they might request a new filter for him, but each attempt had been met with averted eyes and a half-hearted excuse. It wasn't that they didn't care or didn't want to help, but Carlos's status with the foreman had become well-known by that point, and helping Carlos might mean risking their own chance at citizenship—their own chance at survival. Carlos had hoped that an unspoken sense of solidarity might eventually cause one of them to change their mind, but it turned out that a little sympathy wasn't quite strong enough to loosen desperation's grip.

As they passed the 7,000-foot placard, the sign's blinking red light cast his body in a devilish glow.

"So how'd you get your crown?" Carlos asked. Just mentioning the tattoo steeled Carlos's resolve, loosened that knot in his chest a fraction more. "You have to earn it, right?"

The tattoo was enough justification for what Carlos planned to do, but he found himself thinking of his wife and daughter. If they asked him how he'd survived the mines, he'd damn well better have a better answer than, "I killed my young partner because he was a piece of shit gangster that deserved it." Carlos knew the tattoo wasn't some casual sign of affiliation with *Los Reyes*, but he'd sleep better if he had a better grasp on just how rotten Miguel really was.

Miguel looked up from the floor of the grav-lift, his eyes only briefly connecting with Carlos's. It was the same look Carlos's daughter gave him when she'd done something wrong. It was almost like Miguel was afraid of disappointing Carlos with the truth.

"Don't want to talk about it," Miguel muttered, returning his gaze to the floor.

"Oh, come on," Carlos said. "What was it? You rob a bank? Steal some poor kid's bicycle?"

"I said I don't want to talk about it," Miguel growled.

Carlos could feel Miguel reaching his tipping point. He just needed a little push. "Beat up one of your gang's rivals? Burn their house down?"

"I fucking killed someone," Miguel blurted. His tone caught Carlos off-guard. It wasn't boastful. Instead, the words seemed to barely squeeze past the kid's clenched throat.

You rat, Carlos thought. *Probably murdered some poor bastard in the street and took off before you got fingered for the act.* He shook his head and rolled his eyes. "So you ran? Afraid you'd get caught and actually have to own up to what you did?"

"Yeah, I ran," Miguel responded. "But not because I was afraid of getting caught. I ran because I didn't want to have to do it again." He looked up from the floor of the grav-lift and locked eyes with Carlos. It was hard to tell through the thick glass of his visor, but it looked like the whites of his eyes had gone red.

Just the light, Carlos thought.

"My mom died when I was little," Miguel continued. "I never knew my dad. My older brother did what he could to take care of us, but he was just a kid himself. This crown doesn't mean what you think. I know to you it just makes me a thug, but to my brother and me, it was our only ticket to food, a place to sleep, protection. And without money to pay for any of it, it had to be earned one way or another. I'm not proud of it, and if I could have figured out a way to get by without *Los Reyes*, I promise you I wouldn't have done what I did. But it's too late for that now. So here I am."

For the first time that day, Carlos didn't know how to respond, and for the briefest moment, the scorching anger he'd felt toward Miguel waned. He understood what it meant to sacrifice a part of yourself to survive. It was why he'd taken this job in the first place. Digging out the tunnels gave him a path toward a better future with his family. Without it, he'd have been left at the mercy of *Los Reyes* or whatever gang might eventually come along to take their place.

Carlos wished his brain had a console like his exo-suit. If he could, he'd shut it off to stop the thought spiral sucking him in toward its center: if Carlos and his wife had died back in El Salvador, how would his daughter have gotten by? Would he blame her for joining a gang if it meant she would be fed and have a safe place to sleep? Of course not.

Both men fell silent as the grav-lift descended further.

Eventually the staging area, another few hundred feet down, glowed beneath a halo of lights. The sudden glare snapped Carlos out of his thoughts, reminded him of the plan he'd set in motion. The light anchored him. It renewed his sense of purpose—reminded him that it was time to act. Nothing the kid had said had changed anything. None of it made him less guilty. He was a *murderer*, after all. The person Miguel killed could have just as easily been Carlos. It could have been his wife. It could have been his *daughter*.

Carlos squeezed his hands tight enough to crack his knuckles. "When we get down, hop in line for a mag-hammer and a battery bank," he said, reciting the lines he'd scripted for himself. "I'll grab our drill."

"I should get a scanner, too, right?"

"Weren't you saying just a few minutes ago that you were glad to be with someone experienced?" Carlos asked. "If you're gonna slow me down, I can find someone else to hold your hand."

"No, no," Miguel said. "It's fine."

The grav-lift slowed its rapid descent, coming to a complete stop against a set of worn rubber bumpers at the end of the grav-track. Carlos stood, mashed a button to open the grav-lift's door, then stepped onto the staging platform. Ahead were two equipment distribution stalls. Carlos departed without a word to check out their drill and lights.

Standing in line, Carlos felt anxiety swelling in him again, his legs wobbly even with the exo-suit's hydraulic assistance. He watched Miguel approach the check-out for mag-hammers, battery banks, and scanners.

The worker handing out the equipment lifted all three onto the counter, but Miguel only scooped up the mag-hammer and battery bank. As he turned toward Carlos, the distribution worker called out, holding up the scanner.

Please, Carlos thought. *Leave it.*

Miguel shook his head at the worker and turned back toward Carlos. The worker shrugged and replaced the scanner on the rack behind him.

Carlos let out the breath he'd been holding, and he nodded at Miguel.

"We're in tunnel 67C," Carlos said as Miguel approached. "We'll take the elevator down the last few hundred feet, then get to work." Carlos signed for a drill and a pair of high-output LED lamps, and they set off toward a wide elevator platform that would carry them toward a spiderweb of connected tunnels that spread over the fractured reactor cores below.

"Guess the real work is about to start," Miguel said as he and Carlos stepped off the elevator and walked down a dimly lit feeder tunnel toward 67C.

Carlos looked down at his wrist console, the screen red with its relentless warning. "You could say that," he replied. Miguel's murder confession bubbled back into his thoughts, and the familiar anger Carlos felt toward *Los Reyes* simmered once more to life.

<u>8,500 Feet</u>

Carlos enjoyed the drill's unyielding vibrations. It numbed his arms up to his shoulders and drowned out the pounding of his pulse.

Before starting, he'd trained the pair of LED lamps at the craggy rock at the end of the tunnel and plotted out the holes he would drill, mapping out a constellation that would collapse at the precise moment he needed.

Without a scanner's LiDAR and sub-seismic readings feeding into his heads-up display, nothing would warn Carlos of an imminent collapse, but, more importantly, it wouldn't warn Miguel either. Carlos had only his instincts and a thousand hours of muscle memory to guide his hands.

Over and over, he buried the drill's diamond-crusted tip into the rock, watching ribbons of silt drift down as he yanked the tool free. He might as well have been drilling into his own nerves, each hole a gamble that could render his plan useless and snuff out his chances of seeing his wife and daughter again.

As usual, Carlos's thoughts drifted toward El Salvador as his hands instinctively drove the drill into the rock. It was his mind's attempt to find peace amongst the cacophony and danger of the tunnels. He pictured the home he'd left behind: the exterior the color of the sky, the terra-cotta roof gleaming red in the sun.

What should have been a happy memory always led to the same chain reaction of images. He saw the exterior of the home, then the front door, slightly ajar. Next he was striding inside, his heartbeat accelerating, then turning the corner. There, two men stood in his kitchen, guns pointed at his wife and daughter. *Los Reyes.* The Kings.

Even with his eyes focused on the wall of rock ahead of him as he drilled, Carlos could see the crowns tattooed on the men's foreheads in perfect, crystalline detail. He could see the way one of the crowns lifted as the leader of the pair—a rail-thin man with pock-marked skin and bulging veins—conveyed a final warning. With a grimace that twisted into a smile, the man explained exactly what would happen if Carlos didn't cough up the 'protection' money he owed.

"Bang," he'd said, the gun aimed at Carlos's wife, his hand jerking back with an imaginary recoil. Then he pivoted the gun toward Carlos's daughter. "Bang," and another imaginary recoil.

Carlos normally dreaded the memory's inevitable turn, but this time he welcomed it and the familiar way it strengthened his resolve and numbed his fears.

Carlos yanked the drill free of the wall and spun to face Miguel, the crown on his forehead lit with the blue glow of his exo-suit's HUD lights. "You're up," Carlos said, sweat cascading down his forehead and soaking into the undershirt he wore beneath his Tyvek coveralls. He shoved the drill against Miguel's chest hard enough to scratch the pristine paint coating the kid's refurbished exo-suit.

Miguel got that same rabbit-in-an-open-field look on his face, but he traded the mag-hammer he'd been holding for the drill without question.

Carlos pointed at the small section of wall he'd left untouched. "Start here and stay within this area." He traced a square against the rock with his finger. "I'll make sure you're good. When you finish, we'll mag-hammer the shit out of the wall and be that much closer to calling it a day."

Miguel nodded, lifted the drill, and leaned into the rock with the full force of his exo-suit.

With Miguel distracted, Carlos aimed the mag-hammer at the ribbed material covering Miguel's neck. *It'll be over quickly*, he told himself. *Painless.*

He rested his thumb next to the mag-hammer's trigger, its chiseled tip poised to pierce the soft, unexpecting flesh of his young partner. One twitch of his finger, and Carlos could steal the kid's rebreather and bury the evidence beneath a small mountain of rock.

That godawful memory of his daughter sitting at the kitchen table with a gun pointed at her head, her pink toy horse in her lap, played once more in his mind. He sucked in a breath and moved his finger over the trigger, but a sound rang out before he smashed it down.

Miguel was *laughing*.

The sound made Carlos hesitate, and instead of pressing the mag-hammer's trigger, he froze.

Miguel yanked the drill free and turned around suddenly, a smile spread across his face. "My brother would love this thing," he said.

Carlos dropped the mag-hammer to his side. "Your brother?" he asked, stumbling over the words as he feigned an inspection of the mag-hammer.

"Yeah, man," Miguel said. "He got a job doing construction a few months before I left. I thought it sounded horrible, but he said he loved the chaos of the work sites. Something about the way he and the other workers could take a bare patch of earth and create something new." He returned his attention to the wall and resumed drilling.

"Why's he not here with you, then?" Carlos asked, hoping to keep Miguel distracted. "Preferred the company of *Los Reyes* back home?"

Miguel ripped the drill out of the wall, the rock groaning with the sudden movement. "Fuck *Los Reyes*," Miguel said, slamming an armored forearm against the tunnel wall.

Another groan emanated from the rock, and Carlos instinctively took a step back, moving Miguel out of reach of the mag-hammer's tip.

"Me and my brother would be here together if it weren't for them," Miguel said through clenched teeth. "Here we may just be 'backs' but back home people like me are knives. We're weapons—used up until we're dull," his voice cracked. "Or broken." He turned once more toward Carlos and stared at him, his visor fogged with heated breaths.

Through two layers of leaded glass, Carlos inspected Miguel's face. Maybe it was the fogged visor, but the crown on his forehead looked less like ink and more like a brand—a keloid scar marking Miguel's loyalty, willing or not.

The rock overhead released a cloud of silt, and the walls of the tunnel groaned, this time loud enough for Miguel to notice. "That doesn't sound good," he muttered.

Pebbles raining on his shoulders, Carlos dropped the mag-hammer, grabbed

Miguel's exo-suit, and yanked. He and the kid stumbled backward as the rock overhead collapsed with a thunderous shudder. Dust and debris blasted outward, ricocheting off Carlos's suit and smothering the yellow light of the lamps Carlos had set up.

"My god!" Miguel screamed, his legs buried beneath a massive rock and a thousand crumbling stones.

Carlos scrambled to his feet and saw Miguel through the blanketing dust. The red warning light on Carlos's wrist blinked, strobing the walls in crimson. Dust from the collapse plugged the last working portions of his rebreather filter, leaving Carlos only the stale air that remained in his suit.

"Help!" Miguel screamed, his voice rattling the speakers in Carlos's helmet. "I can't move! My legs, man! My fucking legs are stuck!"

Carlos's eyes darted between the mag-hammer he had kicked free of the collapse and the kid. *Not too late*, he thought. He snatched the mag-hammer off the ground and held it over the back of Miguel's head.

"Help me!" Miguel screamed.

Carlos tried to ignore the shrill cries. He tried to focus on what needed to be done. He tried to focus on the hope he still felt at seeing his wife and daughter again. He could end Miguel's suffering. He could take away the kid's pain—save him from another two years toiling beneath a mountain of rock. And in doing so, he could preserve his own future, the one he'd worked so hard to earn.

He breathed hard, sucking in borrowed breaths as he did his best to hold the tip of the hammer steady, ensuring it would strike true, penetrate Miguel's helmet and end the kid's suffering. If he wanted to see his family again, he just needed to pull the trigger—just like he'd done so many thousands of times over the past two years.

But as he worked up the courage to act, that same image of his home in El Salvador crept into his mind, only this time Miguel sat at the table, and instead of the gunman, Carlos himself stood in the center of the kitchen, the mag-hammer pointed at Miguel's temple.

"Fuck!" Carlos screamed, the residual air in his suit thinning. It was all he could say. Torn between self-preservation and becoming the very thing he'd been running from, he froze, unable to act.

None of the tunnel workers signed up to spend their days miles underground next to a nuclear meltdown because it sounded like good work. They were all running from something, and in a weird twist of fate, it seemed Carlos and Miguel were both running from *Los Reyes*.

The tip of the mag-hammer dipped as Carlos's vision swam, his HUD flashing red warnings about his oxygen levels. The chiseled tip hit Miguel's helmet, scraping a shallow rut in the metal, and Miguel let out a moan that snapped Carlos back into reality. "I'm sorry," Carlos muttered, though he wasn't sure whether he was directing the sentiment at Miguel, himself, or his wife and daughter.

He lifted the mag-hammer and pointed it toward the boulder pinning the kid's legs. He pressed the trigger, and the rock shattered into fragments as Carlos's visor fogged over completely. He searched for Miguel's hands, found them, and pulled. The kid screamed as he was jerked free of the debris, his legs mangled.

Carlos wheezed as he dragged Miguel toward the tunnel's mouth, the kid's screams muted as Carlos's consciousness wavered.

When they reached relative safety, the valves containing the air in Carlos's suit finally gave way, popping open with a violent hiss. The suit's fail-safes gave way as his HUD went solid red and his wrist console screeched in warning. Carlos sucked in a lungful of radioactive air, and as oxygen once again permeated his body, his thoughts turned immediately toward his wife and daughter.

Workers in the nearby tunnels emerged, running toward the dust-covered pair at the mouth of 67C.

"He saved me," Miguel croaked as the workers descended on them.

Carlos, supported by a ring of workers, stumbled toward the elevator that would carry him and Miguel to the staging area. As they moved, he heard Miguel whimpering over and over about how Carlos had rescued him.

Carlos drew in another long, quivering breath. As he exhaled, he stared at his hands through tears that welled in his eyes. He knew the kid was wrong. He'd nearly killed Miguel, maybe crippled him.

But then that same old memory came flashing back, only the gangsters were gone, and at the table sat his wife, his daughter, *and* Miguel.

The workers assisting Carlos and Miguel led them toward a waiting grav-lift at the staging area, where they eased Carlos onto the grav-lift's empty bench and laid Miguel down as gingerly as they could onto the floor. Carlos's head swam with each breath, the radiation he inhaled contaminating his cells with poison, and he knew he'd die before he saw his wife and daughter again.

As the grav-lift began its long ascent, Carlos fought off a sudden rush of nausea and leaned over Miguel. "Finish your contract and do something with your life," Carlos wheezed.

Miguel's eyes were wide with pain and panic, but he seemed to understand, though he only nodded in response.

"And the next time you're in a position to help someone, you do it, even if it hurts," Carlos continued. "Because if we don't watch each other's backs, no one else will, and you'll find yourself right back where you started: letting someone use *your* back for *their* gain."

Miguel managed another nod before squeezing his eyes shut and succumbing to the pain wracking his crushed legs.

Carlos sucked in a shuddering breath, sat back against the grav-lift's bench, and slapped his wrist console quiet for the last time. He focused on his breathing, and once more, the sodium lamps became the sunrise cresting over the hills, and the air rushing past his exo-suit became a breeze through his kitchen window.

See Matthew Gomez's story "Right Behind You" online at Metaphorosis.
If you liked it, leave a comment. Authors love that!
Remember to subscribe to our e-mail updates so you'll know when new stories are posted.

About the story

I taught high school English for a number of years, and during that time I wrote a series of lessons based on a story in *The Economist* called "Fields of Tears." The article describes the lengths migrant farm workers from Latin America go to in hopes of earning a better life for their families in the United States. Many of these workers not only endure a perilous journey to get to the U.S., they then suffer through tremendous hardships as part of a workforce that performs back-breaking labor to hand-harvest crops. It's a thankless job, but one that promises at least the hope of a better future. The U.S. has a history of exploiting others' desperation for our gain. For "Right Behind

You," I tried to imagine what that exploitation might look like in a future where an environmental disaster has threatened the safety of the West Coast. Like harvesting crops in the present day, the nuclear disaster has created a job that even our country's most impoverished and desperate won't touch. The story evolved into an investigation of how shared suffering might act as a bridge between two people seemingly at odds. I believe compassion and empathy are our two most defining emotions as humans, and I wanted to see how those feelings might stack up against an individual's instinct for self-preservation.

A question for the author

Q: Do you write with a particular audience in mind?

A: I've tried in the past to write with a particular audience in mind, and each of those stories has failed. In *The Emotional Craft of Fiction*, Donald Maass writes, "The novelist...is not causing readers to feel as the novelist does, or as his characters do, but rather inducing for each reader a unique emotional journey through a story." That line took a lot of pressure off me as a writer by helping me realize I have no control over how a reader interprets my work. That boils down to each reader's life experiences and preferences. Now, I write to entertain myself or work through an idea I find challenging. I do my best to explore ideas in a way I find interesting, and I hope that my readers experience some of the same wonder reading my stories that I felt while writing them.

About the author

Matthew Gomez is the Podcast Editor and Host for Metaphorosis.

Matthew Gomez believes that a story's magic lies in its ability to transpose us into another being's existence, and that the empathy learned there helps us grow in uncharted ways. He serves as the podcast editor for *Metaphorosis Magazine* and is a graduate of Regis University's Mile-High MFA program. One of his earliest heartbreaks occurred when he learned his best friend had lied when he promised hoverboards, like those in *Back to the Future Part II*, would be available to the public in the mid-90's. It's still the litmus test he uses to determine whether we've made it to the future he dreamt of during his childhood.

Find him online at www.gomezwrites.com or on Twitter at @golongria.

The Unlucky Few Who Must Not Cast

J. Tynan Burke

"Hi, my name's Dennis, and I'm magic—"

Dennis stopped before the last word. It didn't apply to him, and he resented the suggestion that it did. Unfortunately, nobody had told the other people in the basement of that run-down Victorian. They looked up from a half-circle of folding chairs, eager for him to finish the line. And finish it he would: doing so was part of the meeting, which he had to attend, by Guild order, that night and nine more times that month, as punishment for his recent magic 'abuse'. Dennis took a centering breath. The air was vaguely moldy.

"...and I'm magic-dependent."

"Hi, Dennis," the basement chorused, out of sync.

Over at the sign-in table, a woman made eye contact. Henrietta, she'd said her name was. Mid-forties, short purple hair, studded collar. Compared to her, Dennis felt decidedly unhip with his Muji khakis and backpack. She gave him a thumbs up; she knew it was his first meeting. Dennis's eye twitched. If magic hadn't been forbidden at MA meetings, he would've cracked open his emergency invisibility potion. Instead he sat back down on his creaky chair, and took a sip of the awful coffee he'd gotten from a dented urn at the snack table. Was it a little late for caffeine? Sure. But he'd need it. He'd been exhausted in the weeks since Phoebe had dumped him, and the meeting was bound to be boring. He planned to stay up late doing spell research anyway.

The man next to him—and it was mostly men, in that basement—stood up. He was dressed like a contractor and shedding the dust to prove it. "My name's Sam, and I'm magic-dependent."

"Hi, Sam," Dennis muttered into his flimsy paper cup.

After everybody had said hello, the facilitator introduced a birdlike woman, "with a reading from the Codex," MA's self-help bible. He passed her a laminated page; she held it in unsteady hands. "How MA Works," she recited. "We are the unlucky few who must not cast. For us, magic is little more than a way to cheat at life. Such a road leads only to destruction. Some end up in prison; some find their bodies wracked with cramps and seizures; some die. Some overindulge and empty themselves so completely, hungry spirits come to fill the void within. The stories we share attest to all of these; they also attest to how good things can become. If you like what you hear, we beg of you to abandon casting and follow our path. You stand at a turning point. You must be fearless in pursuit of abstinence..."

Dennis wanted to scoff. None of that had ever happened to him, but the Guild still thought he belonged with these freaks, just because he'd cast a little while drafting that commodities report. The rule forbidding actuaries from using magic at work was dumb. Who cared? His boss was never going to find out, and it wasn't like he'd acted on some addictive compulsion. The spell had just been an expedient way out of a jam. That was hardly magic dependence.

The woman finished reading and handed the page back to the facilitator, who stepped into the center of the semicircle of chairs. He scratched his careful beard and said he was pleased to welcome that night's speaker, who went by the name of Shisk. Dennis clapped politely as a hulking man came to shake the facilitator's hand. Shisk looked around at his audience. He flashed a smile and tugged down on the hem of his hand-knit sweater.

"My name's Shisk," the big man said, "and I'm magic-dependent." His voice was heavy, either slightly stoned or permanently so.

The room: "Hi, Shisk."

Shisk cocked a wave. The hand he used, his left, moved oddly. Maybe it was a trick of the light. "Hey. So. Who am I, and how did I get here? I can tell you how I got here easily enough: by being a dumbass, then being responsible instead. A few of you probably know what that's like."

Polite chuckles. Dennis rolled his eyes.

"To make the story a little longer. I grew up in northwest BC. My family is

Tlingit. I was seventeen when I got my first taste of *x'aséikw*, and I was hooked. *X'aséikw*, that's Tlingit for—"

Aether, Dennis thought, using the Hermetic term. Shisk finished his sentence with the nondenominational version, *mana*. Not for the first time, Dennis marveled that it could be harnessed by such diverse traditions. The Guild's chaos magicians theorized that human mystics were like blind men trying to describe an elephant: touching on some fundamental truth but failing to see its whole.

"It happened while we were getting ready for my grandpa's memorial party, arranging his stuff for a display. Drums, tools, things from his early life as an *ixt*, a shaman. I'd never put much stock in it... until I picked up one of his old ceremonial masks. What a rush!" He smiled; it faded. "The Guild found out, like they do, and set me up with a master to study shamanism, or what's left of it..."

While Shisk babbled about his training, Dennis's thoughts drifted to his own awakening. It had been similar in spirit. He'd been a freshman in college, wearing too much black and recreationally reading *Magick in Theory and Practice*.

Trying out one of Crowley's rituals had sounded fun, so he had. A small water elemental had appeared in its summoning circle and begun to meander. Dennis had dropped the book in shock; eventually he'd thought to pick it back up and dismiss the creature. Not twelve hours later he'd been contacted by the Guild. They'd sworn him to secrecy and set him up with a master in the anthropology department.

The parallel with Shisk's story was no coincidence. Scooping up the accidentally-awoken was one way the Guild kept magic *sub rosa*. Dennis was also familiar with another way: the Guild monitored its members closely and intervened whenever things threatened to get out of hand. By keeping the magic world self-governing, the theory went, the Guild could avoid telling anything to the actual government. The only problem was that the restrictions could be stupid; sometimes harmless actuaries had to attend boring meetings for people with no self-control.

Shisk went on about how casting had crept into his carpentry business, and eventually taken over his life. Dennis held in a yawn, half bored, half exhausted. How was listening to this guy supposed to help him with his 'problem'? He sipped his lousy coffee, and regretted it.

"Alright," Shisk said eventually. "So that's where I was at in life. I was casting first thing when I woke up and last thing before bed. I'd jones hard for a spell whenever I was in polite company. And I was chronically low on *x'aséikw*. My hands would tremble so bad I couldn't use a saw. My feet would cramp up and stay stuck that way; sometimes I couldn't even get my shoes off. Never did get a full-on seizure, thankfully, but…"

Further evidence that Dennis was not like these people. He'd had some tremors before—who hadn't?—but nothing like what had happened to Shisk. No, Dennis always stopped with a solid amount of *aether* in the tank. Using too much was unpleasant; being half-empty made him feel half-dead. More importantly, it was dangerous, and could make him all-the-way-dead. *Aether* wasn't just fuel for casting; it was also natural protection against spirits. A mage with too little risked possession.

Aether was found in all things, though Dennis wouldn't have been surprised if it were absent from his coffee. It flowed into a caster when they ate, drank, and breathed. Methods of recharging faster were complicated or unsavory. Dennis had never cast enough to need one. Shisk, it seemed, had never been meticulous or evil enough to use one.

"But I still wasn't happy," Shisk said. "Wasting my ancestors' gift on making canoes for lawyers wasn't cutting it. I ended up doing freelance hero stuff. You know: find something wrong in the spirit world, go fix it."

Dennis sighed and rubbed his temple. A sob story from a caster with a hero complex—how *novel*. Heroism never ended well—hadn't Shisk known?

Dennis knew, and his path to learning it had been short. Like most newcomers, he'd been ready to save the world after his awakening. The feeling had lasted about three months, until one evening when he and his master had summoned the wrong spirit. The monster had almost killed them; they had beaten it back, but spent days just cleaning the ichor off the walls, and they never had gotten it all out of the carpet. And for what? If you zoomed out, getting rid of one evil spirit was nothing more than a rounding error.

Shisk's ominous story made Dennis glad that he'd had this revelation when he had. His life would have been very different without it. For starters, he might have actually belonged at this meeting. *There but for the grace of The One...*

"One day I read that a few camping groups had gone missing in the Kitlope Conservancy. This is primeval rainforest, sacred to some, and full of *jeks*—spirits. The sort of place where a missing person can be more than just lost. A quick divination showed me the spot where they'd vanished. I grabbed my toolbelt and headed out.

"Around twilight, I got to the clearing I'd identified. I recognized a threshold on one side, between two tall cedars. A bloodless prickling in my fingers and toes reminded me how little *x'aséikw* I had, but I went through anyway. I was a badass monster-hunter, right?"

Entering the spirit world with low *aether* was even stupider than everything else Shisk had described. On this side of the barriers, monsters generally had to be invited; on that side, all bets were off. Dennis leaned forward, grimly fascinated by the direction of Shisk's story. It was like a good horror movie.

"A river burbled on the other side of the threshold. In front of the river... the *jek* had the shape of a man, except his mouth was too big for his skull, and his eyes moved independently. He was humming to himself, and bending a length of raw wood. Next to him was an unfinished canoe. Its naked ribs seemed like grasping fingers." Shisk illustrated this by making a claw with his left hand. Dennis again noticed something odd about it.

"I rested my hand on the handle of my grandpa's copper dagger, and asked the *jek* about the campers. The jek frowned, and then in a blur he was on me. I stumbled and cracked my head on a rock. Saw stars, heard ringing. He rushed to stand over me, one eye on me, one darting around the clearing. 'You've made a powerful enemy, *ixt*,' he hissed, with a voice like a blade scraping over bark."

Shisk's play-by-play of the fight was brutal. If this had actually been a horror movie, Dennis would have watched from between splayed fingers. Yes, he'd fought monsters before, but he hadn't *enjoyed* it. At least the brutality wasn't senseless— Shisk had been on a rescue mission. That counted for something.

"He wore me down until my hands were so bloody I couldn't even hold the dagger. With all that blood, I'd lost nearly all my *x'aséikw*, too, so I didn't dare cast. I'd never felt worse in my life. Heavy, like my heart was pumping sludge."

Shisk frowned deeply and grunted.

"The *jek* had me pinned against a tree. He was choking me with both hands. But I had one trick left, an old piece of Tlingit lore. I snapped a chunk of sap from that tree trunk and jammed it into my gasping mouth. I mouthed an incantation and grew as sturdy as a cedar. The pressure on my neck... stopped mattering.

"I put my palms on the *jek*'s tattered shirt and willed roots and branches to grow. They tore through him. His whole body shuddered. His hands fell from my neck as he went limp. I heaved in breath after ragged breath, and my throat burned. For a while I sat on the damp leaves and panted. When I finally stood up, it was too dark to search for the campers. They were probably long dead anyway. I hung my head, and my face burned with anger. After all I'd been through, I hadn't saved anybody. I decided to head home."

Dennis felt his body deflate. Shisk had risked his life for nothing. That wasn't how stories were supposed to go, and was far more upsetting than most horror movies. He felt faintly ill.

"When I got close to the threshold, something started probing me, trying to find a way in before I left. Probably the *jek* I'd just fought—killing the skin isn't always enough. I moved as fast as I could, but not fast enough. He—the *jek*, what remained of it—had one last go at me. I don't know how long I spent fighting him inside of myself. Too long. I managed to cram his presence down into my forearm, then my hand, then…"

Shisk held up his left hand and unsnapped what Dennis had assumed was a bracelet. He peeled it from his wrist and palm; his three least important fingers came off along with it. A prosthesis. He wiggled his remaining thumb and forefinger. Dennis's nausea grew; he averted his eyes. "I'll just say it was good I still had that dagger. I put the fingers in a warded Ziploc and hauled ass to the hospital.

"I spent the next few days getting stoned and pretending it had been a carpentry accident. Pretty soon there was a knock at my door. You guessed it: a representative from the Guild. I'd been sentenced to twenty MA meetings. They thought it would give me some perspective, make me less likely to release a dangerous spirit in the future. I was pissed, but in a weird way, I was relieved, too. I obviously didn't have things under control—I'd almost become that *jek*'s next skin. I wouldn't wish that on my worst enemy, so why was I living a life where it might happen to me?"

Shisk said that his path to enlightenment had come through working the steps at MA. Dennis happily sank back into annoyed boredom; Shisk's rock-bottom had been hard to hear about, but the pseudo-religious trappings of 'the program' were easy to scorn.

At length, the shaman concluded. "So yeah, that's my story: how things were, what happened, and how they are now. If I can make it, so can you. *Yan tután, aagáa yéi kgwatee*: have faith and it shall be so. Thank you." Shisk gave the slightest bow and efficiently refastened his prosthesis. After shaking the facilitator's hand, he sat down on a front-row chair. Everyone clapped. Dennis joined them, and not only to be polite: as sermons went, it had been a good one, with a triumphant ending, and a vivid low point that lingered in his mind.

The facilitator opened the room up. People spoke for a minute or two about their own lives. None held Dennis's attention; addict-talk was boring, and all their mistakes were stereotypical. One had tried to cast his way out of gambling debt; another had developed crippling anxiety from too much divination. Instead of thinking about these people's problems, which were not his, or Shisk's story, from which he was still recovering, Dennis focused on nursing his coffee. *How is it even possible for the coffee to be this bad?* he wondered. *It seems like it would take a lot of work. What did they use, fresh scrapings from the street?*

Eventually the facilitator asked them all to stand and link hands. Sam held Dennis's left hand in a callused grip. The man on his right had clammy skin. Dennis mumbled along with a prayer that he vaguely knew: *Grant me the serenity to accept the things I cannot change, the courage to change the things I can, and the wisdom to know the difference.* Then the attendees sat again while the leaders went over administrivia about the next meeting. They collected volunteers for set-up and teardown and refreshments, and Dennis's very first MA meeting was over.

The lights rose. The room filled with the rustling of jackets and the metal noises of latches and zippers. Sitting still in the flurry of bright activity, Dennis felt nailed to his chair, not because anybody was paying attention to him, but because somebody might. He didn't like talking to strangers in the best of circumstances; he definitely didn't wish to right now.

Part of him wanted to spring to his feet and dash to Henrietta, to leave as soon as possible, to get away from this dusty and depressing basement. This urge went away when he saw somebody do just that —somebody who was a twitching wreck. Bad company to keep. With hunched shoulders, he remained seated and checked his email, waiting for Henrietta to finish signing out the other mandated attendees.

Soon it was only him and mingling stragglers. He retrieved his backpack and hoodie from under his chair, then slipped them on. On his way to Henrietta, he slunk between groups discussing happy hour plans and passages from the Codex. Once at her formica table, he produced a folded paper from his backpack and smoothed it out in front of her. She tapped the back of her pen on the gridded form, which was empty except for the first half of the first row.

"What'd you think, first-timer?" she said, looking up at him, pen poised over the page.

"Ah…" Dennis flashed a terrified smile. "Not as bad as I thought it would be?"

She gave a single *ha*. "You know, we get that a lot. Makes me wonder what people expect."

"Er." He swallowed. "Better coffee?"

"I know, right? Jenny—she's on refreshments—she means well, but, yeah. Don't worry, I won't tell." She looked around the basement, then took a crumpled pack of Lucky Strikes from her leather jacket. "Hey, you smoke?"

Dennis's eyes flickered to her pen. She still hadn't written anything. "No. I should get heading home, anyway. The cat'll want dinner."

"Oh, what's her name?"

"*His* name is Oscar."

"Why don't you come show me pictures while I burn one." She glanced at the form. "Dennis."

Dennis gave a low, mirthless chuckle, even though this hostage situation wasn't funny. "You're trying to trick me."

Henrietta smirked. "Is it working? I like to talk to all the newbies. Come on. Five minutes. You'll thank me later." She put her pen into a canvas zipper bag, which she used to weigh down the page, then walked upstairs, waving at Dennis to follow.

Blinking furiously, Dennis stared at the receding woman. *What the hell?* He entertained filling out the form himself, but he didn't know how to fake her initials. Also, it wasn't like him to cut corners; that he'd done so at work recently was the exception that proved the rule. What was he so afraid of, anyway, that he couldn't bear a five-minute chat? He groaned at himself, then hurried over the scuffed hardwood to catch her.

Thanks to the cloud cover, the night was dark and warm, even though a half-rain spat from the sky. Henrietta stopped at a tree on the front lawn. She leaned against the trunk and plucked a cigarette from the pack. She lit it with a Zippo, and the air filled with the reek of naphtha and unfiltered tobacco. Dennis scrunched his nose.

Henrietta pointed the business end of her cigarette at him. "Let me guess. You don't think you belong here."

Dennis opened, closed, opened his mouth. Apparently she didn't like to just talk to newbies, she also enjoyed haranguing them. "Is it that obvious?"

"There's a reason the Guild gives you guys sign-in sheets. Admitting you have a problem is a tough step." She blew out smoke. "Pun intended."

"Yeah." Not planning to take this first step himself, Dennis left it at that. Henrietta smoked; the silence grew heavy and awkward. He had to say something— but what? He supposed he might as well say what was on his mind. "You know, if I'm being honest... I'm not sure casting *is* my problem. I've never had the cramps or gotten possessed or anything."

To his surprise, Henrietta shrugged. The snaps on her epaulets briefly reflected a nearby sodium street light. "Hey, maybe it isn't. Not everybody here's an addict. For some people, like, casting makes their real problems worse. The community here helps them maintain their abstinence."

Dennis half-muttered, "Sort of seems like we didn't hear from any of them."

"Eh. They're not that vocal. Some of them are as embarrassed as you seem to be."

Dennis felt himself blush. Embarrassed, yes; *one of them*, no. "But I don't even have... other problems. Nothing casting makes worse, I mean."

"Hm." Henrietta looked him over, then leaned in. The smoky smell intensified. "Shisk left something out of his story, you know. A year before his life went to hell, he did a first stint in MA. Got sent here for vigilantism; some jackass was robbing houses in his neighborhood, and the cops didn't care, so he used a charm to get the guy to confess on tape.

"We all thought he had a hero complex, and a shitty attitude, too. Nothing was ever his fault. Thought he knew better than everybody else. Could've saved himself a lot of trouble if he'd stuck with the program long enough to get over himself." She rested her back against the tree again and took a leisurely drag. "What I'm trying to say is, the real problems aren't always obvious at first."

"Why would he leave that out?"

"I dunno, vanity? Pretty screwed up, right? I mean, what's the point of speaking if you aren't going to be honest."

"Yeah."

Dennis knew she was trying to manipulate him, but that didn't blunt his

95

surprise. Shisk had had an *early warning* about this? He could have kept those fingers, if he'd only gotten over himself? A vision of the shaman's self-mutilation came to mind. Dennis's stomach ache returned.

Did he have more in common with Shisk than he'd thought? They'd both had hero complexes, however short-lived Dennis's might have been. And they'd both landed in MA because of penny-ante rule violations. It wasn't a perfect parallel, but it didn't have to be to make him anxious. Could his situation escalate like the shaman's had? What sort of violent horrors might be in his own future? Even the less tragic options weren't great; he might become an emotional cripple like the divination addict they'd heard from.

But no, no, of course he wasn't the same as these people. He and Shisk had both broken rules, but the rule Shisk had broken had made sense; Dennis had broken a stupid one. An actuary casting at work was like a driver pumping their own gas down in Oregon. Sure, it was a violation, but it didn't mean they needed Gas Pumpers Anonymous meetings. Just like Dennis didn't need *this* meeting. He should have been at home, having dinner with Oscar. Instead he'd probably have to clean up some passive-aggressive cat vomit. He checked Henrietta's progress on her cigarette. Still half remaining. He grunted.

She held up a palm. "Alright, alright. You heard me out. Thanks. I'll finish quick. How about you tell me how you ended up here, and we can get you on the road."

Dennis sipped his coffee and grimaced. Other than his chat with the Guild rep, he hadn't talked about this with anybody. But if it would help get him home—fine. "I got caught casting at work. A divination. I'm an actuary, so I'm monitored. And here I am." He laughed bitterly. "It's a stupid rule. So I know what next quarter's PNW rainfall will be, so what?"

Henrietta's eyebrows rose. "That's actually kind of a big screw up. You might not want to hear this, but the Guild has those rules for a—"

"I *know* why we have those rules. I just think it's dumb. It's not like I was a cop setting up a pre-crime division. We're talking about lumber futures here."

She looked at him like he'd told her he had not one cat, but fifteen. "Christ, man. If every jerk-off who could read the *I Ching* felt the same way, the foundations of modern finance would crumble. Doesn't sound too bad to me, but I get why others feel different. Even if—"

"Oh come on, nobody cares about—"

"Let me finish." She paused to glare at him, then shook her head. "*Even if* this rule is totally bogus, you knew it was a rule, you knew you were monitored, you did it anyway. What gives? You don't seem like the type to break rules just because you don't like them." She waved a hand vaguely, perhaps indicating his subdued head-to-toe Muji.

"Not every rule is the same!" He pointed at her leather coat, her torn jeans. "You look like you've probably bought drugs before. Does that *mean* anything? No!"

"Maybe you need to talk to Shisk."

"Maybe I need to go home." He folded his arms.

She rolled her eyes. "Easy there, cowboy. God, listen to yourself."

The cigarette's cherry glowed between them as she took a drag. Dennis watched her face brighten and fade. She looked scared. No: worried. For him. He couldn't remember the last time somebody had looked at him that way. It gave him pause.

Listen to yourself. He took a deep breath and slowly released it while he replayed the conversation. His arms fell to his sides as he realized that Henrietta had been right to call him out. He'd been radiating anger and entitlement. He'd sounded like an excuse-making know-it-all, just like Shisk had been at his first meeting. He'd sounded, to borrow a phrase from that earlier recitation, like somebody who used magic to cheat at life. Even his body language had been juvenile and petty. But he wasn't that person—or he never used to be. If he was now, well, that was unacceptable.

"I'm sorry. Let me try again. I hadn't planned to cast that morning. I just... did. I was tired, on an unrealistic deadline... it was an easy out." He sighed; more excuses. His hands fell to his sides. "I was so exhausted. Still am. I haven't been sleeping well lately."

"What's keeping you up?"

"I'll stay up late casting some nights. I know how it sounds, but it's not like that." Henrietta raised a skeptical eyebrow. Dennis scrunched his nose again, but it was from self-consciousness, not the smoke. "I've just been sort of angry. I got—*dumped* isn't even the right word..."

The rain moved from spitting to drizzling. After the first drops struck his forehead, he put his hood up. "I'd been seeing this woman, Phoebe. Pretty casually. She got serious with somebody else, and that was that. I'm sort of mad, but not at her or anything. It just sucks. What do other guys have that I don't, you know? I work hard, I make jokes, I—" He laughed at himself, sunk his hands deep into his hoodie pockets. "I have a cute cat. I dunno. Casting is something I can do that other guys can't. So lately, a lot of nights, I've stayed up late working on a spell. Not like I'll ever be able to show it to a date. Which is silly, since it's just a modified will-o'-wisp summoning, optimized to look nice in a city... I probably sound like a loser."

He shook his head. He barely recognized himself right now. The real Dennis was neither pitiable nor an arrogant prick. Maybe he really did have some things to work out. The cost of not doing so could apparently be dire; he made a mental note to check if his insurance covered therapy. In the meantime, it was possible there were worse places to be than these meetings.

Henrietta smiled kindly. "Sounds pretty, actually." A drop of rain struck the nub of her cigarette, and hissed. She frowned at it, then flicked the remnants into the street. "Let's head back in and we'll get that form signed."

"Okay. Thanks."

He followed her into the old house, into the dingy basement, to the formica table, where his form still rested under her bag of pens. Seeing the mostly-empty sheet of paper reminded him that he'd have to spend many more hours in this musty room, sitting on a folding chair that had long since lost its padding, listening to lectures.

Henrietta crouched at the table. Her knees popped; Dennis winced. She selected a pen from her bag. After scribbling something on his form, she handed it to him. "There ya go. See you Wednesday?"

"Is that the next one? Yeah, I guess." He slipped his form into a document sleeve in his backpack. A few drops of coffee spilled from his carelessly-held cup. "Ah! Crap."

"Careful now, you don't want to waste your favorite drink."

"Ha." There really was no excuse for how bad it was. *Nobody deserves coffee like this*, he thought. *The meetings would be so much easier if we had the right refreshments. Maybe we will next time. Er, not 'we', like I'm a member, but I'm, you know, in the room, and... who am I kidding.*

"Hey," he said, "before I go. Snacks and stuff are handled by volunteers, right? What if I offered to bring... you know... *good* coffee? Wouldn't be much trouble."

Henrietta straightened and looked him over with a curious smirk. "Didn't expect *that*. You'll have to run it by Jenny. I think she's still here. Let's check the kitchen. C'mon."

A few minutes later, Dennis stepped out into the rain and hurried to his car. He opened the door to his Civic and sat on the gray cloth seat. *All Things Considered* came on when he turned the key; Audie Cornish began a story about a blight affecting California strawberries. Dennis pulled away from the curb, then mashed the volume button, killing the sound. He had a lot to think about. That word, *we*, was as good a place to start as any.

See J. Tynan Burke's story "The Unlucky Few
Who Must Not Cast" online at Metaphorosis.
If you liked it, leave a comment. Authors love
that!
Remember to subscribe to our e-mail updates so
you'll know when new stories are posted.

About the story

Addiction treatment focuses on sin—we have programs for alcohol, drugs, sex, overeating, gambling, and so forth. Overindulging in virtuous behavior, by contrast, is called heroism. But that can have negative outcomes, too, especially in speculative fiction—how many times have Marvel heroes wrecked Manhattan, to say nothing of their own bodies? Should people like that have a program, too?

These questions first came to me a few years ago and resulted in two ideas: an accountant who is also a hobbyist wizard, and a twelve-step meeting for magic addicts. I jotted down a line and moved on: "Hi, my name's Dennis, and I'm a wizard."

This year, I finally got around to writing the second sentence, plus a few more after that. I really enjoyed exploring what such a program might look like. What sort of fallen heroes would you meet? And what would the experience be like for somebody who had been ordered to attend? Giving up a vice can be hard enough—what's it like when you're told to give up a virtue? To stop doing the one thing that makes you special?

This being a short story, I didn't have room to explore all the facets of this, but that's okay. I have bigger plans for Dennis, and so does fate.

A question for the author

Q: Duckbilled platypus – result of divine distraction, or alternate universe crossover?

A: The Aboriginal Australians have several theories on the origin of this noble monotreme. Generally, these involve a duck mating with a water-rat. This is true enough, but it leaves out that these creatures were biologically compatible only because the duck in question was from a universe where birds are mammals. The crossover event is believed to have coincided with the formation of the Chicxulub crater. It is unknown what else, if anything, crossed alongside.

About the author

J. Tynan Burke is the Assistant Editor for Metaphorosis.

J. Tynan Burke is a software engineer and writer. He lives in New York City with his husband and their enormous cat, Samwise. When he isn't typing, he plays tabletop RPGs and streams murder mysteries. His dream is to one day be an old man futzing around in the garden. You can find his stories in *Metaphorosis,*

Swords and Sorcery Magazine, and various anthologies.

www.tynanburke.com, @tynanpants

The Great Contradiction

Jordan Chase-Young

Truths can be hard to accept. Long ago, few scholars believed the world was infinite. They were sure its plane had an edge, even as explorers reported continents marching without end in all directions. The world's infinitude made humankind feel insignificant—until we accepted it.

I once felt I was wiser than the ancients. Felt I could embrace any truth. But that has changed. After seeing what I have seen in the black Void above our sky, where the suns make their migrations, I know better.

I learned my lesson the year a fellow scholar asked me to help his research. Normally I would have declined. My work at the Academy of Natural Philosophy in Suyu-Paca, where I've spent most of my life, makes long absences difficult. But I had much respect for the man who sought my insight. And his offer was so generous —three silver links per day of absence— that refusal seemed absurd. Along with his letter, he sent a box of twenty silver links to prove the offer's sincerity: ten for me, ten for my department's seneschal so she might permit my leave.

"How long do you expect to be gone?" The seneschal was a thin woman slowly being digested by paperwork. She sat stiff and stark-lit in the dusty glare of her office window. "You have prentices in need of guidance, lectures I'll have to fill..."

"No more than three months, including travel." I fought the desperation in my tone, knowing she had every right to reject my leave. "But this is Wallaq Squechalwalaq, the finest scientist in the Ecumene. I doubt I'll ever have a greater opportunity to distinguish myself."

"That's all very nice, Atapua, but it's the Academy you're obliged to distinguish.

You serve the Academy foremost, do you not?"

"Of course, Madam Seneschal."

"That is good." She gave me a slow look before signing my writ of leave. "I anticipate your return, knowing you'll have much to show for it."

I gave a bow of gratitude. "I won't disappoint you."

"No," she agreed. "Not if you want your contract renewed."

The day before setting out, I traded two of my new silver links for a sack of bronze ones and gave these to the poor languishing in the streets of Suyu-Paca. Another two I spent on books. Three I sent to my beloved sister, who has been caring for my mother on my birth-continent since my father died. I've long been afflicted by the delusion that sending one's family money can soothe one's guilt for neglecting it.

With the last three links, I rented the healthiest cloudstrider I could find to fly me across the Ecumene. She was a lean beast with broad wings and a long graceful trunk. I had her tusks cleaned, but I washed her brown fur myself. They say grooming cloudstriders is the best way to bond with them.

The trip took a month. I followed one of the Imperial routes, flying twelve hours a day and sleeping each night in a waytown. Miles up, each continent I passed looked as artificial as sculpture. The cities shrank the farther I flew from the core of the Ecumene, eventually becoming sparse dots.

It was hard not to be overwhelmed by the world's infinitude, knowing the Ecumene's sixteen settled continents—not to mention the hundreds of mapped but unsettled ones beyond them—comprised little more than a pebble on a floor without end. If I'd known what lay beyond that pebble, as I do now, I might have been more reluctant to travel.

But I was excited then. And desperate to show the Academy it had chosen wisely in letting me go.

When I arrived, landing a short distance from the tiny windflogged town of Far Eye, Wallaq greeted me not as the highborn I knew him to be, but as a humble scholar, lifting his pointed brown hat for a bow.

"Welcome, Atapua." His deep voice contradicted his small, slim frame.

Handsome, with dark blue skin and silver spectacles, he looked as much younger than my thirty-eight as I looked older, though we were the same age almost to the day.

"Well met, Suz Squechalwalaq." I unstrapped my flying mask and gave a bow of my own.

"Wallaq," he corrected gently. "No point in first names if we don't use them."

I nodded, settling into a more casual mode. "I hope it's not untoward to admit I would have taken your offer for a much smaller sum. My admiration for your work —"

"Yes, yes, likewise." He smiled an easy smile. "We can flatter each other once your steed is stabled and we have hot food in front of us. I've toiled all day and I'm starved."

"Dinner sounds lovely," I said.

I had only a vague idea why he'd summoned me to the remotest town in the remotest continent of the Ecumene. His letter had spoken of *a project to plumb the mysteries of the world* that would require an *interplay of our various strains of expertise in logic and science.* All very cryptic.

But the town looked more suited to shellfishing than science. A stark foil to the warm, teeming city of Suyu-Paca, Far Eye sat on a chilly promontory overlooking a sea. The settlement consisted of nothing more than a dozen rickety jacals sulking beside Wallaq's stone manse. The whole populace served him, I assumed, it being too far from others to have much trade.

As we neared the manse, I caught a muffled din from one of its turret windows, a mix of gruff talk and harsh clanging like in a blacksmith's forge.

"What are you building in there, I wonder?" I asked, my curiosity briefly overcoming my manners.

He gave a casual shrug, his face betraying the tiniest flash of irritation. "Nothing you need to worry about just now."

This only stoked my curiosity, but I had enough sense not to probe.

Dinner was sublime, a large brown vegetable that locals call a forest crab. I cracked its gravied casing with small metal jaws to reach the flesh beneath, relishing each bite as Wallaq's musician, a slender Suyunen woman, played a flute by the crackling hearth.

The manse was huge but not cavernous, thanks to its compact rooms. Only the dining room felt spacious. Large windows looked onto a churning sea beneath a cloudy sky. Hundreds of books filled the walls. Numerous maps lay open on twin fogwood tables. After a sip of wine, I hazarded a guess that most of Wallaq's rooms went to waste, since one could happily spend all their time in this one.

"Correct," he said with a laugh, dismantling his meal with graceful precision. "It's all a bit much for a hermit, I'll grant. But in my defense, I plan to turn this place into an academy someday. When that time comes I'll need every room."

I raised my brow. "An academy? *Here?*"

He shrugged. "Life at the edge of civilization concentrates the mind. And once this continent is well-populated, in a few hundred years or so, this building will be the oldest around. It is good to leave one's mark in stone as well as paper, I feel."

"I suppose," I said, sponging up gravy with a bit of forest crab. I never quite understood folk who cultivated their legacies with such obsessiveness, but perhaps that was just a certain parochialism stemming from my low birth.

"You must be curious why I brought you here," he said with an air of significance.

"Not just food and banter, I trust."

"Alas."

"To be perfectly honest, Suz Sque—er, Wallaq—whatever riddles of nature you think a journeyman scholar like myself can unravel, I have failed to guess."

He pointed his crab-jaws meaningfully at me, staring over his spectacles. "Journeyman in station, perhaps, but not intellect. There, you are my equal."

I was a bit startled by this. He didn't really believe that, surely...?

"The riddle I have in store for us," he went on, "is the greatest of all riddles. The very empress of logical conundrums. Can you guess what it is?"

I shook my head, at a loss.

"I bet you can if you think on it," he said. "But that won't be necessary. Tonight is for food and sleep. Only that. I want you rested for the work ahead."

"No need to convince me," I said.

Shattered from travel, I was eager to engage his ideas—but even more eager for rest. Now that I knew he fancied me his equal—an eccentric delusion, I felt, but a flattering one—I wanted to show him only my sharpest edge.

"Play us Pemac's Fourth Jaunt, in honor of our guest," Wallaq called to the musician, and she slid into the playful piece with exuberance.

Next morning, I met Wallaq at the edge of town. We strolled into the pine forest that cowled a third of the continent, I with a walking stick tucked underarm and he with his small, jeweled hands clasped behind himself.

After a brief interrogation to ensure my sleep and breakfast had been up to his standards, he started in.

"How long did you live on Maipo, may I ask?"

The question took me a little off-guard. Though my subtly striped pink skin marks me as a tribesman of that continent, most folk assume from my Imperial dress and manner that I'm diaspora-born.

"Until fifteen," I said, "when I began to prentice at the Academy. How did you guess?"

He drew a pipe from his satchel and placed a small bit of moss in it. "One can always spot a native Maiponen from the pride they carry with them, thick as perfume." He lit the pipe and puffed it. "I ask because I once spent several months on your birth-continent, studying its flora. Don't these pines remind you of Maipo's?"

I regarded the thick, ribbed trunks and yellowish needles. "Distant relations, maybe."

He nodded thoughtfully. "It intrigues me."

"Why is that?"

"Trees move between continents with an ease animals cannot match. Even cloudstriders, blessed with flight, spread to just four continents before we tamed them. Pines thrive on far more."

I pushed away a low branch with my walking stick. "Seeds are simple vessels. They can survive on the open sea for many days."

"Yes," he said eagerly. "Animals are *not* simple. They need stable environments. Stable food, competitors, climates. Their complexity makes them fragile." He pushed up his spectacles. "Which makes me wonder, of course, about civilizations."

"Are they robust like trees," I guessed, "or fragile like animals?"

"Precisely." He gave a heavy sigh, as if confronting a notion he would rather not. "We seem to be alone in this vast world. Where are all the other civilizations? Did they reach a limit to their growth that no technology can surmount?"

I smiled. So this was the riddle he had in mind: the Great Contradiction. I should have guessed. I knew from my reading that the problem had vexed him for some time.

The question behind the Great Contradiction is simple: *Given the world's vastness, why has no other sapient race been found?*

First, some background. Countless species have been discovered in the sixteen settled continents and in the seas between them. Dozens of those species show keen intelligence. Yet none wield tools or use language as humans do. On the strength of our cleverness, humankind filled its cradle-continent of Suyu in one millennium. From there it spread to two more and filled those in the same span. From there to six others, filling those likewise. And so on. The pattern is clear. From civilization's birth, we have grown exponentially. At current rates, we will fill several hundred continents in a few more millennia. In another few, many thousand.

The riddle arises when one considers that our world, according to geologists, is several million years old. Consider how far a species such as ours could spread in that time. Theirs would be an Ecumene of staggering immensity. Yet we have seen no such thing. Why not? Are civilizations so rare, or do they collapse after a time, done in by wars or plagues or something else?

Ten scholars will give eleven explanations for the Great Contradiction, but Wallaq, I knew, had never found one satisfactory.

"Maybe civilizations are simply that rare," I speculated.

"How rare can they be if they grow exponentially?" he asked. "You've read Suz Huanya Veriyal's treatise on the fate of the world, I assume."

"She thinks the suns will gutter in ten billion years, stranding us in eternal night."

"Many agree with her estimates, including me."

"Her calculations are compelling," I admitted, "however much the thought of a finite future saddens me."

"If she is right, ten billion years await. Plenty of time to thrive. And yet, if our world is millions of years old, as also seems true, there is something deeply strange and suspicious about the timing of our race's emergence."

It took me a second to grasp where he was headed. When I did, I felt a small swell of pride at figuring it out.

"If the emergence of civilization is randomly spaced in time," I said, brushing pine needles from my poncho, "any one civilization should expect to be born near the middle of the world's lifespan."

"Yes." His delight that I could keep pace was palpable. "A straightforward application of Chezaqual's Rule of Banality: *Observers should assume they are not special.* An emergence as early as ours is wildly unlikely."

"Maybe ours is the first," I suggested.

"Or the pessimists are right," he said. "Civilizations reliably destroy themselves."

"A pleasant thought for a pleasant walk."

"I have others."

We returned to Far Eye at twilight. Though my mind was drained and we had made no progress on our subject, I was relaxed and content knowing I'd made a good impression.

"It's quite pleasant," he said, "having someone to discuss these things with. Most folk here, bless their hearts, don't have much taste for high theory."

"They're not deranged, you mean."

He nodded solemnly.

Approaching his manse, I heard that odd clangor from the turret again, but I was too spent to think much of it.

In the dining room, he showed me his collection of maps. These replenished my energy, as beautiful things do. Maps of cities and provinces, seas and continents. Maps of the entire Ecumene, painted and printed and sketched. Even a few crude efforts at charting the lands beyond. Though the atmosphere blurs the Ecumene's margins, even for those who dare skirt the Void's Edge for the highest view, explorers fill the gaps by ranging far and sharing their sketches in the Cartographer's Quarter of Suyu-Paca. Like many restless provincials, I once had ambitions of doing such work, but quickly abandoned them when I considered the merits of living past thirty.

"Have you ever wondered whether it's possible to fly above the Void's Edge?" he asked. He was stoking the hearth as I admired a delicate print of *Heaven's Glory*, one of the oldest maps known.

For a moment I thought I'd misheard. Everyone knew such a feat could not be done. The Void above our world is airless and shatteringly cold. An infinite vacuum where the world's gravitational hold on its atmosphere loses out to the collective gravity of the suns. He knew flight was impossible in vacuum. Was he testing me?

"Folk have tried," I said. "And paid the price."

He held his hands to the fire. "Maybe they went about it wrong. Imagine if we could reach that abyss above the clouds. Reach it and gaze on the world as the suns do. What would we see? Other civilizations?   Things   unguessably strange?"

"Well," I said, my tone dipping into gentle mockery, "if you find a cloudstrider that can fly through the Void, you should go up and find out."

He chuckled.

That night, after a bowl of salty soup and a warm slice of butterbread, I lay awake, steeped in thoughts of flying through the Void as the suns do, millions of miles up. I imagined the world as an endless floor spangled in continents of every hue. I imagined the dark flecks of cities swelling into splotches, swelling and slowly merging into one vast metropolis.

Was this how the Ecumene would look in a million years, I wondered, an insatiable lichen of steel and stone? It seemed inevitable. The thought of such dense, hungry life made me shiver, even as it filled me with a certain grim wonder.

The days passed pleasantly. Sometimes we talked in the dining room, other times in the forest or along the coast. We circled the same ideas, hunting for new insights into the Great Contradiction. A small part of me worried that Wallaq would send me home in disappointment, leaving me nothing to show the Academy. But he was optimistic and seemed indifferent to the lack of progress. He was used to it, he said.

But I was getting itchy. I read all I could from his library, nodding off each night with a book on my chest.

Ten days in, my efforts proved worthwhile. I found a slim, unassuming volume by the scholar Suz Icholaya Inuya, whose name I knew dimly. It was a commentary on the works of the ancient scholar Reva, who made many notable predictions about the fate of civilization based on his study of history. In her book Inuya argued that such predictions were warped by the predictor's context, a bias she called Observer Blindness. A predictor is unusual, the bias said, because their existence depends upon historical accidents they cannot know. The future will not resemble the past should those accidents cease to shape events.

I bridled. If she was right, then how was any prediction possible? Her reasoning held a fatalism that threatened to unravel all efforts to solve the Great Contradiction. Yet it had merit. I granted that.

After pondering her work a bit longer, I stumbled upon an idea so interesting I almost sprang a muscle rushing to my desk. I wrote furiously before the thought could fade.

The idea was this. Suppose some span after the world's beginning, say ten million years, civilizations merge to engulf the world. Afterward, no room will remain for new civilizations to form. All of nature will have been used up. Thus anyone pondering the Great Contradiction, like myself, must inhabit that slice of cosmic history before such a phase-change has occurred.

This was the solution to the Great Contradiction.

My heart raced. The implications overwhelmed me. With some statistical juggling, my insight let me calculate not just when humankind was likely to meet other civilizations but, through parallel reasoning, how far away they should be.

Carried away by my excitement, I felt an urge to share my insight immediately. I put on my slippers and hurried to Wallaq's room, wending through a labyrinth of torchlit corridors, my head humming with adrenaline.

En route, I heard an odd, metallic tapping that seemed to come from a nearby stairwell; I assumed it was the sea wind rattling something outside the manse and went on.

Reaching Wallaq's chamber, I was disappointed to see no candlelight below his door. I had a thought to wake him. Surely he'd forgive me under the circumstances. But common sense restrained me. I would tell him tomorrow, I decided, and headed back to my room.

I paused at the stairwell, puzzled by that strange tapping. On a lark, I followed the sound to a higher level, realizing it was the din from the turret I'd been hearing. The building's thick walls had kept the noise from reaching my chamber.

As I neared the source, a shut room at the end of a corridor, I grew amazed that any stone could muffle such a racket. And more amazed that anyone would be tinkering at this hour.

Four or five voices wove through the clanging. They spoke Imperial Suyunen, so I was able to parse the few words I caught. It seemed the builders were making a machine, or several machines, but I struggled to tease out much more than that. One builder complained of a deadline; another reminded him how much they were being paid. A third mentioned the Void.

My pulse rose. What did their work have to do with the Void? Did the deadline have to do with me? Did Wallaq want the project done before I went home?

I would have listened longer, but one of the builders mentioned turning in for the night. That was my cue to return to my room.

I lay in bed for hours, pondering Wallaq's mysterious project even more than my discovery. Piecing together all I'd heard, I began to suspect what he was building.

We broke fast near a tide pool several miles up the coast. I wanted to discuss my thoughts right away, but Wallaq insisted on eating first.

We munched sour seedpods while watching the wildlife, sleek gray animals with otter bodies and cuttlefish heads. They were foraging dark strands of kelp that had tangled on the rocks. The air was cool and salty.

I was nervous. What if he found my ideas absurd? What if they were? I needed something to take back to the Academy, something to impress the seneschal. Neglecting to renew my contract had been no idle threat.

But I was getting ahead of myself. I took a breath to still my nerves.

When we finished eating, I proposed my explanation for the Great Contradiction.

Wallaq puffed his pipe in silence. My nervousness grew as the silence stretched. I wrung my hands, waiting for him to tear apart my theory. Waiting for him to realize I wasn't his equal, I was a fraud and he'd been a fool to bring me here and—

"They build them clever on Maipo," he said, nodding. "I think you may have solved it."

Sighing inwardly, I veiled my pride with calm detachment. "Writing a treatise will take time. Weeks, at least. Then there is the Academy's process of review, which my theory may not survive."

"If it is correct, we will know soon enough."

"What do you mean?"

"What I mean," he said, "is we will fly as high as needed to search those distances likely to harbor other civilizations. Thanks to your calculations of how far away they should be, we have a notion of how high we must go."

My hunch was right. "You're building a device to leave the atmosphere."

"*Devices*," he said proudly, appearing to enjoy the emotions on my face. "Shall I show you?"

"God's mercy, yes."

The first thing he showed me resembled a suit of armor with a barrel fixed to the back. Twin tubes ran from the barrel to a glass-visored helm. The builders massed at the edge of the workshop watched with prideful protectiveness while I studied their work. The craftsmanship of the steel surpassed anything I'd seen in my life.

"The armor's insulated against cold," Wallaq said, "and retains air spectacularly well. The air is stored in that barrel."

"Compressed?"

"Yes. Four and a quarter-hour's worth. One tube brings air into the helm. Another draws carbon dioxide into a chamber at the barrel's base, where a sieve of minerals traps it."

"Ingenious."

He showed the second object, a bulky canvas-and-steel harness containing a parachute and joined by ropes to several winches. He pulled a cord to make the parachute retract.

"These ropes tether the voidfarer—my term—to four attendants' cloudstriders. Once you're done surveying, the attendants winch you back into the atmosphere, where you then release your parachute for easy wrangling."

"How does one enter the Void to begin with? The air is too thin at the Edge for cloudstriders to near it."

"That's the best part."

He showed the last device, a cross between a saddle and a catapult. It too was jellyfished with ropes and winches.

"It wasn't easy, calibrating the force needed to fling one past the Edge without breaking the tethers." He twisted one of the saddle-catapult's knobs to tense the device, then pulled a lever. The catapult portion sprang upright, making the table shudder. "As you might expect, a fair number of wooden dummies are hurtling through the Void as we speak."

I shook my head in awe. "How long have you worked on all this?"

"For fifteen years, I've tested things of this kind, but only the past three have borne fruit. In a few days, the work will be done. Thanks to you, we know how high the voidfarer must rise and thus how long the tethers should be. I'll be making the inaugural journey myself."

I was startled. "If I'd known that was your plan—"

"The pressure would have hurt your concentration," he said, and he was right.

"Can't you send someone else? Someone whose death, God forbid, would not be so...?"

Tragic? Disastrous? Words failed me. There is a certain callousness in assuming anyone's death could be less terrible than anyone else's, and an extra callousness in suggesting he put another soul at risk in his stead. Yet I could not help myself, knowing what the Ecumene would lose if he perished.

He shook his head. "I cannot. I could not live with others dying for my vanity. Less altruistically, I wish to be remembered as the first soul to reach the Void. After all my struggle, I cannot let another claim that legacy."

"Ah." *Legacy. Of course.*

"Naturally," he said, waving his hand, "you will be free to make a survey of the Void as well. It is only fair."

The thought chilled me. I was intensely curious about the Void, like any scholar.

But I was also a bit of a coward. I did not like to put myself in danger when I did not have to.

Disappointment came into his eyes at my hesitation, subtle but sharp enough to sting my pride. "My devices have been tested exhaustively. I assure you, they're quite safe. Are you not eager to see your ideas vindicated?"

"Yes," I said with a nervous swallow. "Of course."

He smiled and clapped my shoulder. "Good."

The evening he returned from his survey, I was deep in my treatise, my head heavy with numbers and hands smudged with ink. The sound of cloudstriders through my open window tore me from my work. I put on my boots and hurried out of the manse.

Wallaq removed his helm. His face was flushed. His eyes looked far away.

"Wine first," he said.

I did not argue.

We drank in the dining room. A servant brought tubers diced over black moss and drizzled in oil. He touched none of it. Just gazed at the darkening sea, hearthlight playing over his spectacles like an errant thought.

I felt him struggling with emotions and did not speak for some time. Finally I could not help myself. "What did you see?"

"I don't think you'll believe it," he said. "I did not, at first."

"Tell me."

He spread his small hands on the table like an augur laying out bones.

"Truthfully, I'm not sure. Only that they must be the work of a sapient race."

"They?"

"I will tell you. But you must promise something." His tone went low and his gaze turned grave and steady. "You must promise to believe that what I saw is what I saw, believe I am telling you the truth as I perceived it. Do you promise?"

"I promise," I said, forcing calm into my tone even as my heart banged my ribs in anticipation.

He gave a nod and looked down at his hands. "I saw tendrils."

"What?"

"Do not speak until I'm finished." I shut my mouth. "I saw tendrils, on the horizon. Black tendrils that have captured a sun."

He paused as if summoning the memory took physical effort. I learned forward slightly, the hair on my neck standing straight.

"*Digested* may be more apt," he went on. "They rise hundreds of miles above the atmosphere, these tendrils, their contours just visible in their captured sun's red light. The land at their base is paved in darkness. A great darkness that throbs with strange lightning."

He kept looking down as he spoke, as if afraid to find disbelief on my face.

"That is what I saw," he said. "Whatever race built them must hold unimaginable power. But what frightens me most is their—strangeness. They seem nothing like us, Atapua. Their works look so sterile, so cold."

At last he stared at me again, and his expression was such that I knew—simply knew—he was telling the truth.

A dozen emotions warred in me. There was joy in my vindication. Feelings of awe and wonder. There was curiosity, confusion. Most of all, dread. A dark ashplume of dread that settled over my soul in slow waves.

The scholar in me had expected this news, or something like it. The rest, the human part, had not. Had never fully absorbed the implications of my theory.

"These—tendrils." My voice was brittle at the edges. "How far away?"

"Millions of miles, at least."

"What else did you see?"

"The light of the captured sun blocks much of the horizon. I did spy other things—a mountain that pierces the atmosphere, for instance—but nothing so clearly artificial as these—these suneaters. Even at that height, one can only see so much."

It is rare to hear a thing which you know will change humankind forever. This was such. I considered it carefully.

The first thing that came to mind, small and selfish though it may seem, was that my contract at the Academy would never lapse now that I was tied to the most important discovery in the Ecumene's history. I would be raised to masterhood overnight, no doubt, and would never want again for respect or money. A delicious thought.

My next thought was less so. When the populace learned what Wallaq and I had discovered, how would they react? He and

I were jaded scholars, not easily flustered, yet this discovery put fear in both of us. Surely ordinary folk would fare worse. Much worse. Along with their peace of mind would go a certain innocent confidence in the rightness of their beliefs. A hundred gods would be cast down. The very gearwheels of human morale might shriek to a halt.

For the first time in my life, the fate of humankind no longer felt abstract. It felt personal.

"Do you still wish to go up there?" he asked.

I nodded. "I must see the truth, however much I fear it."

The air-suit was warm and heavy. The tube filtering my breath tasted like salty leather. The visor bent sunlight strangely, spraying brief rainbows. Too cumbersome to carry unaided, my telescope was joined by several articulated rods to my breastplate.

The saddle-catapult creaked each time my cloudstrider beat her wings, creaked and shuddered as she pushed higher into the heavens. The ropes tying my saddle-catapult to my four attendants—who flew in a wide, ragged ring around me—began to tauten as they cranked their winches.

I'd never flown as high as I was now, perhaps fifteen miles above land. The clouds had thinned to milky threads. The nearest sun, a glut of golden flame now migrating over the continent of Yaro thousands of miles to my left, outshone by several orders of magnitude the next-nearest, whose path lay countless miles outside the Ecumene.

By now my terror had faded to resignation. If I was to die, at least I would die in service to the truth.

But I was *not* going to die. Wallaq had survived. I would survive as well.

Up I climbed, until the sky's blueness grew brittle. Once my saddle-catapult's tethers were taut enough to support me, I uncoupled the saddle-catapult from my cloudstrider, who descended back toward Far Eye.

Now was the moment.

I licked my lips, bracing myself. I twisted the knob of my saddle-catapult, felt it tense, and pulled the release lever.

The Void's blackness crashed over me.

I was weightless, rising like a bullet shot into a vast night, my air-suit's own set of tethers, mercifully joined to my attendants far below, following me ever upward.

Once free of the atmosphere, I saw the world as no human but Wallaq had seen it: a bright mosaic chased with the white of clouds and the gray-blue of seas. Continents shone like topaz and amethyst and emerald.

I rose and rose until the ropes wrenched me back, and then I started falling, then rising again, my motion slowly stabilizing as my kinetic energy dissipated, leaving me held by the collective gravity of the suns. My guts did a slew of gymnastics all the while. Wallaq had warned me about this part, but it was no less unpleasant for that.

As my stomach stilled, my senses sharpened. The world's enormity filled me with a cold loneliness, a stifling vulnerability. The thought of my ropes snapping sloshed thick in my head, but I shook it away. I had to concentrate, I told myself. Had to focus or I couldn't do what was necessary.

I looked through the telescope and scanned the horizon.

After about ten minutes, I found it.

I'm not sure what I'd been expecting. Perhaps part of me hoped Wallaq had misperceived.

I dialed the aperture with gemcutter care. *There.* Countless continents away, untrammeled by atmosphere, sat a red sun tangled deep within scores of black tendrils.

My body reacted several ways at once. My pulse rose. My skin began to slicken with sweat. I prayed a Maiponen prayer I had not used in two decades of godlessness.

The tendrils were artificial. Unmistakably. Their trunks had a metallic sheen and their forking branches a flawless symmetry. The violet lightning at their roots surged in orderly grids instead of stochastic squiggles. It was like the disembodied eyeball of a dead god, cataracted with rot yet still smoldering with divine energy. A voice in me said to look away, said this was not something I was meant to see. But I could not.

I found Wallaq at his hearth, winecup in hand. He and wine had seldom been apart of late, and his slight slur suggested this was not tonight's first drink.

"Cursed together," he said, cup raised in greeting. "Cursed with the truth of our insignificance."

I am not much of a drinker, but for once I understood that timeless thirst for oblivion. I poured a cup and sat beside him.

"It was more incredible than I expected, and more terrible," I said.

"Do you regret it?"

I shook my head. "Yet the sight will haunt me, Wallaq. For a long time."

"As it will me."

I could not sleep for two nights.

What I saw in the Void changed me. In my religious youth, the high god of the Maiponen faith had seemed too distant to matter in worldly affairs, and so I was free to imagine that humankind determined its fate, a freedom I carried happily into adulthood. It gave me comfort. A sense of purpose.

Now I knew the truth. Gods were no myth. Humankind was not the cynosure of reality. It was only a small—perhaps transient—participant.

What will befall humankind when it meets the sun-eaters? I wondered with fear in my marrow. When the ambits of both civilizations converged, in who knew how many centuries, would there be war? Mere devourment? What happens when a god meets an insect?

I could not begin to guess, no matter how hard I tried, and this tortured the part of me that yearned to know all.

I finished my treatise a few days sooner than hoped. Wallaq helped me revise it a dozen times, scrawling notes in each draft, smoothing the language. I knew it was the most important thing I'd ever write. Maybe the most important thing *anyone* would ever write. Yet I felt detached from it. Stripped to cool spareness, my words failed to touch a tenth of the import of what I sought to explain.

Words are dead things. Some truths can only be seen. Yet words were all I had.

Done with the work, I had my first deep sleep in days. I did not look forward to leaving Far Eye, not a bit, but I had struggled long and hard with the treatise and I was glad to have it behind me.

The night before I left, we feasted. We ate butterbread bowls brimming with molten beans, crackers tucked in mashed spicecorn, plump mauve vegetables marinated to soupy softness. We had devil's dowry, a red Yaronen fudge laced with a subtle euphoric. We drank and talked deep into the night. My pleasure was tinged with sadness, knowing my taste of the highborn's life would soon be over, along with my new friendship.

A servant opened a finely wrought folding-case on the dining table. Inside was a long chain of silver links. I'd never seen so much money in one place.

"Thank you," I told Wallaq. "Thank you."

He waved aside my bows of gratitude. "You earned every mote. Truthfully, after all your help, I should be paying you double."

"There's always time to repent."

He smiled. "Good try."

We clinked cups and drank. He'd saved his best wine for last.

"I'll miss your company," he said. "It will be hideously dull around here without our discussions."

"I'm sure you'll be plenty busy fending off scholars when they come swarming to verify our discovery," I said.

He winced at the thought. "Or those who've come to vent their hatred over it. No doubt I'll have to quadruple my security. Are you concerned for your safety?"

I shook my head. "Only worried for the Ecumene's sanity. Worried what will become of faith and purpose, what will become of folks' trust in the Empress to protect them, what will become of the things that hold a civilization intact."

"We're scholars, not priests," he said testily. "Our loyalty is to truth, not the comfort of three billion souls. Best not forget that."

This rankled me. Was he so distant from ordinary suffering that he could not appreciate the pain our discovery would bring?

"*Your* loyalty may be to truth," I said as calm as I could, mindful of the emotions my wine was trying to draw from me. "Mine is to civilization."

"The two are not at odds," he said.

"Perhaps, in this case, they are."

He frowned. "What are you suggesting, precisely? That publishing this treatise would be a mistake?"

I laughed. Wallaq, I saw then, was the emotional equivalent of a child. Not in any simple or disparaging sense—merely in the sense that he could not appreciate any considerations outside his appetites, which in his case were wholly intellectual. He was a child, yes, who ate knowledge for breakfast, lunch, and dinner, and to whom morality was a bowl of tasteless vegetables. I knew such people at the Academy, of course, though none half so intelligent or resourceful, so it had been easy to overlook this tendency in him.

He'd been wrong to suggest I was his equal. I could never be his equal, as I did not have the childlike singlemindedness that his cast of genius requires.

"What I am saying," I said flatly, "is that publishing the treatise *might very well* be a mistake. What I am saying is that I might spare us both a good deal of misery by—well, throwing the damned thing into the fire."

I gave the roaring hearth a small salute with my winecup.

His face showed no amusement. "You're drunk, friend. Don't say such nonsense."

"I'm serious." My annoyance was bubbling to anger. I set down my cup, intending to walk to the table where my treatise lay, but he must have sensed this because he placed a gentle hand on my arm before I could stand.

"Listen," he said. "You underestimate people." His hold was surprisingly firm for such a small man. "The truth is inevitable. If you were to burn that treatise, which of course you won't, it would only be a matter of years before others learn what we've learned. Don't you see? You cannot burn the truth, Atapua. But people will adapt, as they always have."

His soft voice held reassurance. His face was calm, understanding. Yet there was a marked tension in him, as if he were ready to do anything to stop me from burning that document.

He was right, as he so often was. He was right. I could not have burned the treatise no matter how drunk I got. I was proud of my work, unreasonably so, even as I feared it.

"Yes," I sighed, relaxing a little. "People will adapt."

I did not wholly believe it, but it was not beyond possibility either. People accept many painful truths. Mortality, for instance. Injustice. Why couldn't they accept the truth of the sun-eaters?

Perhaps.

See Jordan Chase-Young's story "The Great Contradiction" online at Metaphorosis.
If you liked it, leave a comment. Authors love that!
Remember to subscribe to our e-mail updates so you'll know when new stories are posted.

About the story

Earlier this year, my friend Robin Hanson shared a provocative paper exploring the possibility that humankind's early emergence in cosmic history, and the apparent absence of other civilizations in the universe, may be a selection effect due to most of the universe's future being under alien control (https://arxiv.org/abs/2102.01522). I puzzled over how to turn this insight into a story and finally settled on a fantasy parable, as I felt that would be easier to fit into a few thousand words. The Ecumene is one of many SFF settings that've been collecting dust in my head, so I was grateful to have a story to set in it.

The most challenging aspect of the tale was plugging in concepts like the Fermi Paradox, Copernican principle, and selection effects while keeping the language accessible and the pacing smooth. I ended up trimming a lot of Atapua's analysis to avoid bogging down the piece. I also fleshed out Atapua's emotional world more and more with each draft, hoping to capture the complex emotions that scientists can have upon reaching a breakthrough with ambiguous consequences.

Though the setting is fantasy, the story is pure SF; it's about the fun and often scary ordeal of uncovering a difficult truth about reality. I share some of Atapua's anxieties about that process, but I tend to side with Wallaq's view that people are good at adapting to hard truths. What about you?

A question for the author

Q: Can beautiful things be funny?

A: Humor's a funny thing. Though many writers say humor's tougher to write than drama, funny stories have always been harder to sell than dark ones. If I asked you to name the most beautiful story ever written, I bet you'd pick a drama, maybe even a tragedy. Beauty and darkness feel oddly close, whereas humor seems somehow more frivolous.

Hence attempts to call comics "graphic novels" to make them more respectable.

Where do these associations come from? Maybe humor is mainly about incongruencies in the world, such as paradoxes in language or social relations, whereas beauty hinges more on congruency, elegance, symmetry, order. Humor may also be time-serving and culture-bound, beauty timeless and universal. Still, it's a rare masterpiece that doesn't have a dollop of mirth to lessen the gloom, and nature, the greatest masterpiece of all, is often wickedly funny. Look at a blobfish lately?

About the author

Jordan Chase-Young is the Proofreader for Metaphorosis.

Jordan Chase-Young is an American SFF writer living in Australia with his wife and their stable of cyborgized battle koalas. He's kind of obsessed with the future: What will it look like? Where will it lead? His first published story, "Shards", appeared in the July 2020 issue of *Metaphorosis*. Since then, his stories have appeared in *Unidentified Funny Objects 8, The Colored Lens, McCoy's Monthly*, and the Zombies Need Brains anthology *When Worlds Collide*.

ebookofthenewsun.wordpress.com, @jachaseyoung

Copyright

Title information

Metaphorosis November 2021

ISSN: 2573-136X (online)
ISBN: 978-1-64076-211-4 (e-book)
ISBN: 978-1-64076-212-1 (paperback)

Copyright

Copyright ©2021, Metaphorosis Publishing.
Cover art ©2021, Lauren Ring

"Treedom" © 2021, A.J. Cunder
"Right Behind You" © 2021, Matthew Gomez
"The Unlucky Few Who Must Not Cast" © 2021, J. Tynan Burke
"The Great Contradiction" © 2021, Jordan Chase-Young

Authors also retain copyrights to all other material in the anthology.

Works of fiction

This book contains works of fiction. Characters, dialogue, places, organizations, incidents, and events portrayed in the works are fictional and are products of the author's imagination or used fictitiously. Any resemblance to actual persons, places, organizations, or events is coincidental.

All rights reserved

All rights reserved. With the exception of brief quotations embedded in critical reviews, no part of this publication may be reproduced, distributed, stored, or transmitted in any form or by any means – including all electronic and mechanical means – without written permission from the publisher.

The authors and artists worked hard to create this work for your enjoyment. Please respect their work and their rights by using only authorized copies. If you would like to share this material with others, please buy them a copy.

Moral rights asserted

Each author whose work is included in this book has asserted their moral rights, including the right to be identified as the author of their respective work(s).

Publisher

Metaphorosis
a magazine of speculative fiction

Metaphorosis Magazine is an imprint of Metaphorosis Publishing
Neskowin, OR, USA

www.metaphorosis.com

"Metaphorosis" is a registered trademark.

Discounts available

Substantial discounts are available for educational institutions, including writing workshops. Discounts are also available for quantity purchases. For details, contact Metaphorosis at metaphorosis.com/about

Metaphorosis Publishing

Metaphorosis offers beautifully written science fiction and fantasy. Our imprints include:

Metaphorosis Magazine
Plant Based Press
Verdage

You can also find us:
@MetaphorosisMag, @MetaphorosisRev,
@Metaphorosis
www.facebook.com/metaphorosis

Help keep Metaphorosis running by supporting us at
Patreon.com/metaphorosis

See more about some of our books on the following pages.

Metaphorosis

a magazine of speculative fiction

Metaphorosis is an online speculative fiction magazine dedicated to quality writing. We publish an original story every week, along with author bios, interviews, and notes on story origins.

We also publish monthly print and e-book issues, as well as yearly Best of and Complete anthologies.

Come and see us online at magazine.Metaphorosis.com

Metaphorosis: Best of 2020

The best science fiction and fantasy stories from *Metaphorosis* magazine's fifth year.

Metaphorosis 2020

All the stories from *Metaphorosis* magazine's fifth year. Fifty-two great SFF stories.

Metaphorosis: Best of 2019

The best science fiction and fantasy stories from *Metaphorosis* magazine's fourth year.

Metaphorosis 2019

All the stories from *Metaphorosis* magazine's fourth year. Fifty-two great SFF stories.

Metaphorosis: Best of 2018

The best science fiction and fantasy stories from *Metaphorosis* magazine's third year.

Metaphorosis 2018

All the stories from *Metaphorosis* magazine's third year. Fifty-two great SFF stories.

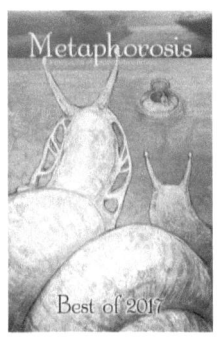

Metaphorosis:
Best of 2017

The best science fiction and fantasy stories from *Metaphorosis* magazine's *second* year.

Metaphorosis
2017

All the stories from *Metaphorosis* magazine's second year. Fifty-three great SFF stories.

Metaphorosis: Best of 2016

The best science fiction and fantasy stories from *Metaphorosis* magazine's first year.

Metaphorosis 2016

Almost all the stories from *Metaphorosis* magazine's first year.

Plant Based Press

plant
based
press

Vegan-friendly science fiction and fantasy, including an annual anthology of the year's best SFF stories.

Best Vegan SFF of 2020

The best vegan-friendly science fiction and fantasy stories of 2020!

Best Vegan SFF of 2019

The best vegan-friendly science fiction and fantasy stories of 2019!

Best Vegan SFF of 2018

The best vegan-friendly science fiction and fantasy stories of 2018!

Best Vegan SFF of 2017

The best vegan-friendly science fiction and fantasy stories of 2017!

Best Vegan SFF of 2016

The best vegan-friendly science fiction and fantasy stories of 2016!

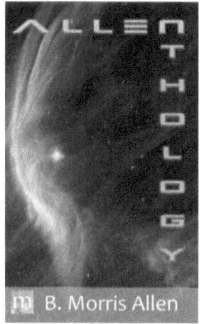

Susurrus

A darkly romantic story of magic, love, and suffering.

Allenthology: Volume I

A quarter century of SFF, including the full contents of the collections *Tocsin, Start with Stones,* and *Metaphorosis.*

Verdage

Verdage

Science fiction and fantasy books for writers – full of great stories, often with an additional focus on the craft of speculative fiction writing.

Reading 5X5 x2

Duets

How do authors' voices change when they collaborate?

A round-robin of five talented science fiction and fantasy authors collaborating with each other and writing solo.

Including stories by Evan Marcroft, David Gallay, J. Tynan Burke, L'Erin Ogle, and Douglas Anstruther.

Score

an SFF symphony

What if stories were written like music? *Score* is an anthology of varied stories arranged to follow an emotional score from the heights of joy to the depths of despair – but always with a little hope shining through.

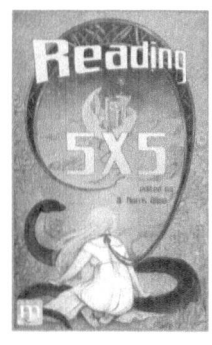 

Reading 5X5

Five stories, five times

Twenty-five SFF authors, five base stories, five versions of each – see how different writers take on the same material.

Reading 5X5

Writers' Edition

Two extra stories, the story seed, and authors' notes on writing. Over 100 pages of additional material specifically aimed at writers.

Vestige

Novelettes, novellas, and novels by Metaphorosis authors.

www.ingramcontent.com/pod-product-compliance
Lightning Source LLC
Chambersburg PA
CBHW050449110726
47899CB00003B/870

* 9 7 8 1 6 4 0 7 6 2 1 2 1 *